GUN LORDS OF TEXAS

The South had lost the war. But now the Seven were back in Texas following the surrender, and there was plenty of land for everyone — that is, until a fortune in gold and a gang of killers showed up to threaten the peace. That was when Cole Shannon and his men strapped on their guns again and decided that this was the war they would either win or go down shooting . . .

MATT JAMES

GUN LORDS
OF TEXAS

Complete and Unabridged

LINFORD
Leicester

First published in Great Britain in 2007 by
Robert Hale Limited
London

First Linford Edition
published 2008
by arrangement with
Robert Hale Limited
London

The moral right of the author has been asserted

British Library CIP Data

James, Matt
    Gun lords of Texas.—
    Large print ed.—
    Linford western library
    1. Western stories
    2. Large type books
    I. Title
    823.9′2 [F]

ISBN 978–1–84782–320–5

Published by
F. A. Thorpe (Publishing)
Anstey, Leicestershire

Set by Words & Graphics Ltd.
Anstey, Leicestershire
Printed and bound in Great Britain by
T. J. International Ltd., Padstow, Cornwall

This book is printed on acid-free paper

1

Shannon's Brigade

The nation was still weeping over the graves of its Civil War dead as the ragged band of riders attired in the tattered remnants of Southern grey rode slowly on south through the deepening dusk.

The guns were stilled, the ink upon the surrender documents had dried. Yet to the ears of seven war-weary veterans there still lingered the echo of the cannon, and each man believed he could still, from time to time, faintly scent the gunsmoke on this dry Texas wind.

For between them they had seen it all: from Bull Run to Mill Springs and from Shiloh Schoolhouse to the mayhem of Gettysburg and Atlanta.

'How much further, Cole?' grunted

the bearded ex-grenadier as the timbered hill rose before them.

'Why, as far as it is, I reckon, Jack.'

'Goddamnitall, if a man asks a straight question he deserves a straight enough answer back, don't he?'

Brawny and hard, Jack Quade was naturally tough as old bootheels. Yet the man was also weary to the bone that Texas twilight. All were — Quade, Riley, Harney, Brothers, Quill and Morgan — even tall Shannon himself.

The remnants of the fighting unit once known as Shannon's Brigade were close to total exhaustion as dusk came to this remote corner of Texas. But that didn't mean they might get to slack off or even relax at the dying end of another long day — or even have a querulous query answered, for that matter. Or at least to their leader, it didn't.

This time Shannon merely indicated the way ahead and a peeved Quade spat between his horse's ears, muffled a curse and stoically kept riding.

They were veterans who had fought for the Cause as fiercely as anybody could for four long years of shot and shell. Yet now it was all over, even this loyal band of brothers often appeared reluctant to take orders. But because it was Cole Shannon who at times still appeared to be pulling rank, they mostly just grumbled and grouched, then let him get away with it.

There was more than blind loyalty behind this seeming deference.

For they had come home to Texas, and it was this that bolstered the spirits of the six, and Shannon himself as much as any man.

The journey had been a long one via Tennessee, Missouri, Oklahoma and now mighty Texas. Riding horses sporting the US Army brand and with two mules toting their camping gear, the south-west-bounders had for endless weeks wearily followed the remotest trails, the lonely hills and the most difficult canyons on their long diagonal journey across the Lone Star State.

3

They had avoided all towns as any battle-weary man would at such a time, day after day soaking up the peace and the vast and healing silences.

And every mile, distant Paiute County was the magnet that continued to draw them across the endless plains of south-west Texas.

In Paiute County, a place deliberately selected as a place none had ever seen, they planned to draw rein finally and settle down to begin living like sane men again. Or so they constantly promised one another as the endless horse miles stretched away behind in their dust.

In Paiute they hoped to be able to erase names like Fort Pillow and Cemetery Ridge from memory and perhaps even get to forget the dead they'd left behind them.

This ultimate destination, Texas, had been voted for unanimously by all seven for one reason and one only: the maps of Texas indicated that Paiute was about as far as a man could travel to distance himself from the war, yet still remain within the Lone Star State.

But even Shannon was showing plain signs of exhaustion by the time they reached willow-fringed Cracker Creek, hitherto just a speck on the map Pop Harney toted in the hip pocket of his Levis. Had they been normally alert they would never have virtually stumbled upon those exhausted figures stretched out in the long grass beneath the trees. By the time they realized others had staked out a campground across the creek, all they could do was rein in and stare.

It was gloomy beneath the scattered piñons but enough light filtered through to outline something strangely unsettling to battle veterans — the silhouette of two mules harnessed to what appeared to be a small wagon cannon.

Shannon counted three sprawled figures there beneath the trees. He nodded. The odds — if they should prove important — were shaded his way.

As the dust of their horses slowly drifted across the stream, the campers suddenly became aware of their silent presence. Just as they were stirring, a fourth figure emerged from the brush in back of the trio toting an ancient rifle in the crook of his arm.

Seven former Rebel guerrillas tensed as the men leapt to their feet, wildly grabbing up their guns. And now the campers could be clearly seen they became instantly identifiable as a breed all too familiar to survivors of the great war.

They had called them Scavengers up north where the cannon raged. Vermin with loyalties to neither North nor South, they preyed upon the victims of war, were to a man cut-throats, thieves and pitiless vermin who profiteered from chaos and human misery.

Cole Shannon remained outwardly calm even as he signalled to the others to put them on full alert.

Then that fourth hardcase stepped forward beneath the willows to glare across at him with sudden hostile recognition.

'Shannon!'

The face and voice jolted Shannon's memory back to a war-torn day in Alabama where he'd chanced to come face to face with this redneck border raider.

They had traded shots that day, the guerrilla leader and the scavenger.

Instinctive natural enemies then were such again instantly now as the outlaw cursed and jerked up his weapon. 'Gun 'em down,' he roared. 'This you see here is Shannon's stinkin' Brigade, boys!'

Shannon's Brigade!

To the desperadoes the name conjured up images of a deadly enemy, while to the vets it was a stirring reminder of who they were, and how they had fought as one from old and awful battlefields where men such as Quantrill, Wild Bill Wilson and Hannerman Jones had once preyed upon the weak, defenceless and the unarmed.

All verminous scum — exactly like these.

In an instant the seven had cogged

back in battle mode, even though the surrender at Appomattox lay ten long weeks behind them now.

Shannon's gun was first to roar — and he was shooting to kill. He was supported instantly by his troop as Morgan, Quade, Riley, Harney, Quill and Brothers hit ground and cut loose just as though it was Bull Run or Shenandoah all over again.

It was almost like a battle between men and boys — battle-scarred veterans of a hundred campaigns versus the human scum of the borderlands.

A gaunt figure hurled himself belly flat into the long grass as Shannon's belching .45 erupted from less than fifty paces distant.

The scavenger aimed his piece, yet failed to get a single shot away.

Suddenly he jerked upright, smiling strangely down at the rusted shooter dangling unfired from his fingers. Blood trickled from between his jaws. He stumbled forwards to plunge headlong into the murky stream and floated away, face down.

In the seconds it had taken the scavenger to die the veterans had raked the creek bank opposite with a volley of such ferocity and accuracy that by the time Shannon moved to support them it was all over.

Silence.

His men had mastered many skills over the years, but what they did best of all was kill.

It grew intensely quiet along Cracker Creek with drifting tendrils of gunsmoke weaving ghostlike though the afternoon trees.

It was hard to believe men could die so fast. It was almost as though they might have been simply too weary to stay alive any longer.

The seven regarded themselves very much now as ex-soldiers, yet were anything but surprised to find they retained their lethal skills.

There was no hint of triumph, no celebration as they rose silent in the deepening dusk. Just the one question.

Why?

Why had the vermin gone for guns against such obviously superior odds? Certainly their leader had identified Shannon from the past. But surely that in itself wouldn't have tempted even someone of his low calibre to risk a shoot-out as he'd done?

This thought continued to preoccupy Shannon as he moved to stand grimly over a bullet-riddled corpse that continued to leak dark blood into the thirsty grass.

He started as, from a short distance away, Digger Morgan raised his Colt and shot one of the mules crippled in the firefight. The lanky Australian stepped across to the surviving mule, grabbed up its harness and began murmuring to it soothingly. The man from down under hated badmen but loved horses.

Suddenly big Jack Quade hollered: 'One here still breathing, Cole!'

Shannon went quickly to the scavenger's side and dropped to one knee.

Plainly it was all over for the man, drilled through the sternum. He stared up from the buffalo-grass, a man close to death yet defiant to the last.

'Only wish I'd claimed you, Shannon . . . I'd almost be happy to be going now if I had . . .'

'We can all dream, tenth-rater!' snapped Courtney Riley, leaning over Shannon's shoulder while the others grouped around in a circle. 'So, why'd you start shooting, loser? What happened? You just get weary of living?'

Bitterness glazed the dying man's eyes.

'Bastards . . . We had all them years livin' hard, half-starving and all outta luck . . . then . . . then almost at the very moment we strike it lucky . . . you . . . stinking sons of bitches bob up outta nowhere and . . .'

'Yeah, yeah, we've all been bad-named by experts before.' Shannon's face was stone. 'Just remember, Dunbar started in shooting and all we did was defend ourselves, pilgrim.'

11

The man suddenly twisted his head at a sound to see Pop Harney fiddling with the overturned cannon which had been hitched to the mule team before gunfire stampeded the animals.

His expression intent, Pop was reaching down into the barrel after something, this causing the man lying in the grass to swear feebly yet with blasphemous bitterness. None paid him any heed, for at that moment Harney withdrew his hairy arm from the cannon muzzle, drawing forth a sack of something that appeared disproportionately heavy in relation to its size.

'Plunder!' guessed Gar Brothers, bounding across the creek to the old man's side. He jabbed Harney in the slats, took a look at what the man had hauled forth, then waved his battered campaign hat back at the group. 'It's gold . . . some of it is leaking out, by God!'

And gold it proved to be.

As triumphant and exuberant as Robert E. Lee's conqueror at Appomattox Courthouse on the day of shame and surrender, Pop Harney made his bow-legged way back to the group clutching a double handful of heavy gold coins. Several dropped in the bloodstained grass where Brothers, Riley and Quade instantly pounced upon them. There were single- and double-eagles, all stamped with the mint seal of the United States of America.

'The . . . that damn gun barrel's crammed full of them, Cole,' Harney gasped disbelievingly. 'And those renegade bums were hauling it around like trash. Must . . . must be thousands of dollars' worth, all told.'

'General Shelby's war chest?' speculated Gar Brothers. 'Cole, that's what it could be, man. Remember, we heard about it back at — '

'Shelby never saw this much gold in his life,' contradicted Quade, who knew a great deal about such matters. 'I very much doubt if even Sherman himself might've done, for that matter.'

Turning a glittering double-eagle in

his fingers, he peered down at the bloodied figure in the grass.

'We've got your loot, pack-rat!' he taunted with a broad grin. 'All of it — see!'

The dying man closed his eyes with a groan. But then his eyes reopened to mere slits to stare bitterly at the coin which Quade now held close to his face.

'So . . . we've lost the last hand now . . . ' he panted, as though speaking to himself. Then with a terrible effort he hauled himself up on to one elbow and reached out for the coin with trembling fingers. Fresh blood pumped from the cruel holes in his body with the effort, yet he seemed beyond pain now.

'I truly believed . . . after all those years . . . that we had our reward coming. Damn you all to hellfire . . . it was like the gods was smiling on us when peace was declared exactly at the time me and Ned's boys jumped that bunch of wore-out Bluebellies and found that crummy cannon stuffed with a thousand times more than we'd ever dreamed of. We . . . we were making for Mexico when you . . . you . . . dirty . . . '

His voice cut off and they thought he was gone.

But Morgan jabbed him with his pipestem and his eyes blinked open to focus one last time upon on the expressionless bronzed features of Cole Shannon.

'The least you can do is tell me how you tracked us, Shannon, you motherless bastard. Just tell me where we slipped up . . . '

'You're wrong,' Shannon growled. 'We didn't know about any gold — '

'You . . . you'll see just how wrong you are when . . . when Ned . . . Ned . . . '

Suddenly the man was gasping for air and his wild-eyed stare went beyond them. He reached out as though sighting somebody in the distance. Once more he struggled to speak again, at last succeeded, 'S-sorry, boss, but we done our best . . . '

Staring eyes glazed over. He was dead by the time Shannon uncoiled to his full height.

'That name again,' he mused grimly. 'Ned. Ned who . . . ?'

'Does it matter?' queried Kit Quill, youngest of the bunch and the most dangerous one. He chewed a straw, and shrugged slim shoulders as the others looked at him. 'Ned, Tom or Parnell Ichabod? Whoever owned it don't own it any more. It's all ours . . . right, Shan?'

Shannon made no reply. He guessed it was exciting to come by a huge swag of gold that seemed it could have belonged to virtually anybody or nobody. But already he could see problems ahead if they kept it . . . He interrupted that train of thought with a frown. What did he mean — 'if'? Just looking at the faces encircling him told him that some of them at least already had it invested, blown at the gambling-tables or frittered away on some blousy dame whose breast measurements far exceeded her intelligence.

Then he found himself thinking, 'Wonder if this mightn't well be part of President Davis's last shipment from the coast destined for General Hooton in the Wilderness? They never found that . . . '

He shook the thought away and looked at Morgan whose eyes looked the size of double-eagles.

'How much do you figure, Cole?' the hardcase asked breathlessly.

Shannon did a little totting up in his head then said with forced casualness, 'Could be as much as ten — twelve thousand, mebbe . . . '

The six who had fought alongside Shannon through four years of one of the bloodiest wars in history stood dumbstruck as the full magnitude of the incident began to sink home.

As members of a special forces saboteur brigade fighting continuously behind the enemy lines, the men who had ridden under Shannon throughout four years of shot and shell were now

17

the sole survivors of a Southern unit which had at one stage peaked at thirty men.

Most of that time the outfit had been engaged in desperate and unpublicized actions behind Union lines. As a consequence of their anonymity and other factors, they had seemingly been lost in the shuffle when it came time for post-war honors and rewards, had eventually headed back West pondering, as so many a veteran did, whether it had all been really worthwhile.

Now like a bolt from the blue a fortune had simply tumbled into their laps!

It was grinning Gar Brothers who was first with the question now preoccupying all.

'Well, Shan, old boy, where does that leave us hard-luckers? You wanna tell us that?'

'I see it all!' young Kit Quill said excitedly before the other could respond. He threw supple arms wide and stared up into the Texas night sky with popping eyes. 'I see me a grand hotel . . . and

I mean grand. I see silk sheets and pretty women and someone to come shave me every morning — '

'Well, there'll be no squandering for me, lads,' broke in Digger Morgan in his broad Australian twang. 'I just reckon I'll be using up my cut to pay the boat fare for my Libby to come and join me from old Sydney Town. And you just imagine how surprised she is gonna be to hear the old Digger finally struck it big after five years away from home.'

Old Pop Harney, always the optimist, chimed in next, painting a word-picture of himself as the major business tycoon and maybe even mayor of some great town like Midland or Odessa. Then even sober and black-bearded Jack Quade was heard to laugh like a boy as he declared that, for the first time in his life, he intended to invest the grand sum of thirty dollars in a genuine pair of Star riding-boots.

It was Quade who eventually realized that one man was not taking part in the general excitement. Nudging Riley, he indicated a pensive Shannon where he stood apart staring thoughtfully down upon the dead man in the tall grass, still turning that coin over and over between his fingers.

The others grew aware of his preoccupation and one by one fell silent.

At last Jack Quade spoke up.

'Something on your mind, Cole?'

Shannon swung his gaze to the Kansan, then cleared his throat.

'Just thinking that standing up to our knees in dead men doesn't seem the right time to be kicking up our heels, I guess.' He paused, then added: 'Matter of fact, I reckon we should all be digging and not sky-larking right now.'

'Digging?' challenged Riley. 'You can't mean you want us to plant these Yankee scum, do you?'

'There are no Rebs or Yankees here tonight, Court,' Cole replied. 'Just Americans, like us.' He turned away. 'So let's get busy. We'll get them in the ground, get packed and get gone. I had my fill of sleeping around dead men and don't plan doing it again.'

Some grouched, others cussed, a couple even appeared to agree with him. But it was testimony to Shannon's authority that even if griping and cussing, every man set to work with his saddle shovel, ripping holes in the soft prairie earth. They reassured themselves as they labored, that by the time they left this place and the stink of gunsmoke far behind, Cole would be back to his old familiar self again.

But he wasn't.

While the bunch worked on in the half-dark, Cole Shannon sat keeping look-out from a grassy knoll, still with that same double-eagle in his fingers.

He was finding it difficult to handle this stroke of 'luck.'

Four years of murder with mostly never enough to eat — then suddenly a bonanza of yellow gold! A kindness or a curse? He was musing as the others eventually returned from their grim chore.

He sighed and uncoiled to his feet. Only time would tell.

He took no part in their animated conversations before blanket time came around. By the time they eventually settled down and watched his silhouette passing slowly to and fro before the fire, it was a puzzle for Morgan and Pop Harney to see their leader was acting exactly as they had seen him do countless times during their four years together, when for one reason or another he'd considered the Brigade to be in danger.

'Plumb curious,' old Pop sighed sleepily. But then the veteran of three wars settled his scarred head into his pillow to dream of high times and rye whiskey, of silk shirts and glossy women.

And a cannonful of yellow gold . . .

2

Pueblo

They were still waiting for Shannon to reveal his plans as high noon approached next day. Annoyingly, he showed no sign of doing so as he sat his saddle in the shade of a sprawling cottonwood grove on a lonely hillside.

Yet the leader was busy even if he didn't look it, as his gaze followed the high plume of dust that had risen in the wake of a stagecoach they'd sighted spanking across the flats towards Pueblo in the far distance.

The big black horse which he called Ulysses tossed its head in impatience but the rider didn't appear to notice.

Shannon had always been a thoughtful man but the others reckoned he was overdoing the long and pensive silences since they'd encountered both violence and gold back trail.

'What's he waiting for?' burly Gar Brothers growled at last, sweat rolling off rugged features.

'Doubt he's waiting for anything,' opined Jack Quade from beneath a bullet-holed sombrero. 'My guess is he's just thinking is all.'

'About what?' Kit Quill was young, outspoken and impatient by nature. 'Now we're in the money, what's to think about?'

'Shut your griping, junior,' Pop Harney said tetchily.

'Who's griping, you old cowpat?' the kid shot back.

'Be quiet, both of you, damnit!'

The voice of authority was that of Courtney Riley. The former Kansan gunslinger was no older than Quill but there was a vast difference in their characters.

For Quill was still a kid, while nobody would ever think of Riley in that light. Riley was vain, proud, and lightning with a Colt .45, some claimed possibly even better than Shannon, although that could be stretching it a little.

'How much did we say, again?' Shannon grunted after a silence.

'You know, damnit.' Jack Quade grinned, at his side as usual. 'Ten thousand. No need to act coy about it, man.'

'Lot of money.'

'Could also be a lot of trouble, I'm thinking.'

'Keerect.' Shannon nodded, and sounded troubled.

Following the slaughter back trail the band had sat around in silence watching Pop lovingly count the gold into neat little piles and he'd seen the hot excitement in their eyes.

He also detected the occasional glint of something else; the first unmistakable hint of greed in eyes of men, few of whom had ever seen more than a hundred bucks at one time in their lives before.

It was a bonanza, for sure. But that

didn't mean a man should not worry about it some.

He grinned at a sudden thought. Pop Harney claimed Cole had spent more time during the war looking out for his 'boys' than he had done in dodging Yankee bullets. 'Mother-henning', Pop had called it sometimes.

That came of having been an orphan kid, he guessed. When you at last found yourself a family you tended to grab hold of it even if it mightn't be the real thing.

'OK, OK,' he said as Pop got ready to say more. 'We're going in.'

Everybody cheered. Sure, the gold was something huge and exciting. But what every man craved even more in the wake of the surrender and the long trek back home to Texas were the everyday things, or at least what had been everyday before four long years of murderous insanity.

Normality.

A town with women and kids in it and beer and whiskey when a man wanted them, not when some stiff-assed officer said you could or could not. In that mood they were like kids again, even old Pop, arrogant Riley and big Jack Quade. And rather than delay them further with a boring lecture on how to act and not draw undue attention to themselves in there, Cole just swung his arm forward and the bunch was off like kids when the afternoon bell had sounded.

Soon they were racing. And Cole Shannon was amazed to find himself shouting wildly in his horse's ear and deliberately cutting Digger off when he tried to get past him as they stormed neck-and-neck across a grassy knoll.

Gar Brothers won the final dash into the main street accompanied by yells of 'foul' from Courtney Riley and the curses of a genuinely outraged Kit Quill.

The uproar subsided when they found themselves in a broad and dusty main street with a sizeable crowd of startled citizens assembling to stare in alarm as seven well-mounted strangers reined in before the big saloon, bristling with belt guns, saddle rifles and here and there a big black shotgun.

'Hey . . . it's all right, folks!' Shannon yelled, waving a friendly hand. 'We're just travelling through and we got a little anxious when we lost our trail across the flats, so we kind of hurried along — '

He broke off as the sound of a creaking axle and plodding hoofs sounded behind him. Everyone turned sharply as two ugly mules rounded the city hall corner hauling a battered old cannon in their dust.

'Just a souvenir, folks!' Digger Morgan reassured. 'From the war, y'know. You hear about the war way down here?'

Someone laughed, someone else yelled an insult. But the ice was broken and when a weedy figure sporting a lawman's star emerged to order the mob to break it up and get about their business, the bunch began genuinely to relax — until Brothers and Quade led the sudden rush for the King John saloon.

Although Pueblo looked like paradise under a good coating of alkali to the seven, it really wasn't much of a town even by Texan post-war standards. Situated upon a flat, white alkali step, it had about it an air of neglect, an island of desolation encircled by vast burning flats with the heat waves shimmering over the scarred and rocky hills beyond the plains, the granite outcrops.

An ugly town wrapped in sloth and indifference. That was Shannon's assessment as he lowered his first cold one at the gloomy bar.

Even so, it still seemed the ideal place where seven travel-weary and newly rich former men-of-war might get to relax for the first time in an eternity. And maybe — most important of all — might even get to agree on exactly what shape the brigade's future would now take in the view of its change of fortunes.

The towners continued to act curious, as well they might. But the way he figured, if they could simply get by quietly without some fool suddenly whipping up a drunken argument about the war — still very much on minds from coast to coast — then the stopover could only do them all a power of good.

'Good liquor, barkeep.' Shannon grinned, draining his glass. 'The same again for me and my brigade.'

'Brigade?' the fat little barkeep said as he reached for bottles and glasses. 'That what you boys are?'

'Keerect,' chimed in young Kit Quill with a hint of challenge in his manner. 'Shannon's Brigade' was the name they'd fought under and it would be hard ever to shed it. The drinks were lined up and Shannon, Morgan, Quade, Riley, Harney, Brothers and Quill toted their glasses to a big round table in the centre of the room where they proceeded to send them down with a flourish then sat waiting for the welcome warmth to caress mind, body and spirit again.

'How long, oh Lord, how long?'

Brothers sighed dramatically. Then lifted glass to lips and drank again.

Soon they were almost relaxed.

The post-war plan of the Brigade had always been to remain together, travel to south-west Texas and take up at ranching.

Shannon himself had likely always been the plan's staunchest supporter. For he had no kinfolk, no idea of who his folks might have been, nor just what Western mystery had resulted in a two-year old toddler being found abandoned one chilly dawn in Amarillo bawling for food, attention, anything he could get.

From such an unpromising beginning he had managed to survive as a street kid who ran errands, minded folks' small children and, later on, handling odd jobs better than boys twice his size and age. He was breaking wild horses on a big Texas ranch at fourteen and scouting for the first of the huge westbound wagon trains of the fifties long before he started shaving regularly.

Two years as a successful wagon master saw him looking to a solid future at the time the cannon of Fort Sumter reverberated around the world, and instead he enlisted in the Army of the South in the first weeks of the war.

The best thing about the war had been the Brigade — the name his superiors had tagged his special unit of scouts and troubleshooters which he was destined to command through four years until the surrender.

These men were his brothers, the only ones he had ever known, or would know. Yet deep down, he sensed it was unrealistic to imagine the surviving seven might simply keep rolling along together for ever in peace-time as they had done in war.

Yet that was exactly what had happened thus far, and he was beginning to believe it might continue. Or at least he had done so before Cracker Creek.

He had always envisioned them setting down roots in some region they'd never seen before, somewhere far enough away from the war and its memories while still remaining in the mighty state of Texas.

With map and pin they'd selected the town of Boiling Fork situated in Turkey Track County. It had a hick country sound yet to them it had also sounded just like a place where a man might get back to being just a man again — not a killing machine.

He saw no reason why this plan should change now simply because Lady Luck had smiled. Yet the question nagged internally; had they survived the war only to be destroyed by gold? Tasting his next with relish Cole knew that they simply must thrash this out as they'd done with far bigger and more hair-raising problems in the war.

But not yet.

Certainly not on this once-in-a-lifetime day when each man at last felt free simply to celebrate and unwind any way he damn well pleased.

For rugged Gar Brothers, after taking

the sharp edge off his thirst with three straight shots with the others, it meant securing a pint bottle of sourmash, ordering a king-sized meal, then retiring to a quiet corner where he set about stuffing his big body full of corn liquor and prime vittles in a way he had been unable to do in years.

Kit Quill, the gun-quick kid with a hint of the loco in his make-up, didn't drink as much as the others, but had himself a fine time dancing with ferocious energy with a succession of pretty partners and bribing the ancient fiddler with free drinks whenever the tempo of the music slackened off.

Digger Morgan and Jack Quade sat down before huge platters of steak and beans washed down with generous quantities of cold beer, after which they were invited to sit in on a poker-game. Digger was noisy and lost his ready, Quade was the big, quiet winner.

Courtney Riley, who somehow always managed to appear dapper and debonair even in dusty trail rig, shared food and wine with a busty girl who found him the best-looking of the 'family'. He'd assured her they were a family of Southern cotton millionaires heading for the Rio to wreak bloody vengeance upon a wealthy Mexican clan for defiling his sister's purity and good name.

Old Pop Harney was content to sit slugging rye in a roomy window seat where he could watch the horses tethered outside, while he toyed with a shiny golden double-eagle in his pants pocket.

Although often the centre of attention in any situation involving the whole bunch, Cole Shannon remained odd man out here in Pueblo. Not that he didn't try to join in. He did. He stood at the bar for a considerable time, drinking purposefully. For he wanted to get drunk, if not rolling drunk, then at least happily so.

He even waved aside the frequent offer of company from busty girls in order that he might concentrate on his liquor. He sampled some rum, switched to tequila, then back to the rum again.

The sun slid down past deep windows that were shuttered against the western glare, and the level of his rum bottle steadily fell. Yet for some strange reason he remained sober.

Some time later Digger Morgan got into a fight with a big-nosed local and deliberately allowed the bum to beat him just so the girls would fuss over him later.

Kit Quill, after exhausting every girl in the place with his machine-gun routines on the dance floor, jumped upon the bar and performed some clever acrobatics while doing sleight-of-hand tricks with his sixshooter.

Meantime, Riley had lost a wrist-wrestling match to a 300-pound blacksmith, then easily won an impromptu shooting match out back against Quill and Jack Quade, when at least half-drunk.

Cole Shannon watched it all, enjoyed it all — and remained dead sober.

At first he tried to convince himself

that the reason he couldn't unwind was because he was out of practice. When that failed to convince he thought he must still be living in war time, still half-expecting the sudden crash of cannon and still too much on the alert to allow himself loosen up and get properly soused.

Yet when he found himself still drinking and still stone sober at nightfall the realist within forced himself to face up to the truth at last.

It could only be the gold.

He set his shot-glass down upon the bar and studied his reflection in the cracked mirror and finally admitted to himself that his secret fear was that he might be presiding over the terminal disintegration of Shannon's Brigade.

And the perceived enemy which might cause this disaster was not Confederate shell nor back-shooter's bullet, but rather two heavy canvas sacks crammed tight with Yankee gold.

He poured himself another little

drink and prayed this wouldn't be so. Then he decided the matter had to be solved before they rode from Pueblo next day.

★ ★ ★

Three hours later and he still hadn't announced his big decision!

Shannon shook his head with annoyance as he sat quietly in a corner of the slowly filling barroom, glass before him and cigarette in hand. He might as well admit it, he supposed. He was too damned nervous to call for the big parley.

For what if they failed to agree, and the big discussion he felt they must have should result in the breakdown of the bunch?

If that prospect wasn't scarier than, say, the spectacle of a squadron of Yankee cavalry bearing down on you while their cannon blasted the daylights out of you from some other quarter — then he didn't know scary.

The rest were all there enjoying themselves while their leader instead found himself brooding on how this had all come about; himself, how it had all started for the leader of Shannon's Brigade . . .

He hadn't set out to lead the Brigade or anything else for that matter, he mused. Looking back he saw that leadership had just seemed to gravitate to him naturally, whether it had been as top hand on a ranch, bossing a thirty-Conestoga wagon train . . . ultimately leading on to his ranking as officer in command of a special services unit working mainly behind enemy lines in the War Between the States.

He grinned at a thought.

His *segundo* Jack Quade was also a leader — of sorts. Jack knew how to lead men, just as he knew how to brawl, drink, or blow up enemy troop trains with dynamite. The reason he'd never risen higher than 2IC was simply his temperament. The big man just loved to fight. That was an asset in wartime but could prove a liability in peacetime.

Gar Brothers was quite likely the most powerful physical specimen of the bunch, an easy-going country boy and a master with horses, while his good pard, Digger Morgan, the Australian, had always been the bunch's raconteur, forager and often peacemaker when his fellows in the Brigade fell out.

Young Kit Quill was a quiet and immensely talented boy, wise beyond his years, while by sharp contrast, his saddle buddy was just about his opposite in every way that mattered.

Top shootist Courtney Riley was born rich and privileged but had lost his entire family and fortune in the siege of Atlanta. Vain, volatile but gifted, Riley could be difficult and even dangerous at times, which made him a very different Brigader from Pop Harney.

Prematurely gray at forty and worn and weathered, genial Pop was still as tough as teak, and frequently acted as peacemaker when members of the bunch might fall out or get to kick over the traces. Pop was genuinely amazed to have survived the war and was now determined to weather the peace — if his six good pards would let him.

His outfit.

Seven men of different temperaments and backgrounds facing a future irrevocably changed by riches.

Deep down, Shannon didn't believe they'd ever get a line of where the gold had come from or who might have the right to claim it. The country was still in turmoil and would be for a long time to come.

So, displaying an uncertainty such as he'd never been guilty of during four years under the Yankee guns, he promptly announced a postponement of the debate and recommended instead they should turn the night into the first genuine blow-out and booze-up they'd had in four years.

He was cheered to the echo and the night that followed proved memorable in every way that counted.

Even so, Shannon couldn't believe how the morning he was dreading seemed to come around as fast as it did.

3

Tumbleweed

It was the drums that awakened Shannon early next morning — Apache war drums if he was any judge — thudding louder and louder right outside his rooming-house window.

He snatched his .45 from its holster as his bare feet hit the floor, yet even as he rose to his full height and tenderly fingered his forehead, he was remembering he was no longer out in the wilds but in the heart of Pueblo. So — how come war drums?

He drew his window curtain and cursed as sand and dust peppered his window momentarily. Then the haze abruptly cleared to leave him gaping.

Directly below him a mad-eyed horse was bucking across the hotel yard trying to dislodge the insane

43

horseman bouncing in the saddle.

He shook his head in disbelief, convinced he was hallucinating from too much rye whiskey. But it was all too real. The wild horse belonged to the liveryman who, during last night's boozy ribaldry, had offered a ridiculous sum to any man who might prove capable of breaking 'Monster' to saddle and bridle.

It was Digger Morgan who'd taken up the challenge. Shannon brushed his hand across his eyes and looked again. Yes. Digger right enough. He'd always suspected the Australian horseman might be a dime short of a dollar. Surely this was proof of it.

'No brains and real happy without them,' he groaned, turning away.

It was amazing the difference a wash, shave and solid breakfast could make. By the time he was working on his second cup of strong and black on the hotel's back porch an hour later he was feeling almost normal again.

But, thinking clearly now, he realized

nothing had changed. The sole topic of conversation on the porch focused on the gold and their future plans and it wasn't until they insisted he join in that he knew straight talk could be avoided no longer.

He was amazed at just how straight he sounded when he voiced his honest fear that he did not believe they could survive their dramatic changes of fortunes in the way they'd always planned.

They were shocked, even the fire-brands. Everybody started in talking at once and the wrangle that ensued continued until exhaustion set in — by far the most serious clash in the Brigade's four-year existence.

This was what he said; what he was thinking was vastly different. But they were not to know that, and when they recovered from the shock and started in attacking him, the more heated they became the more Shannon shook his head and looked grim. Yet inside he was exuberant. For his grim predictions were simply a ploy he felt it necessary to make in order to cut through all the big talk and dissension and uncover how they really felt about the gold and the dramatic changes it might bring.

But he kept pressing.

'Think on this,' he declared as they paused for breath 'That gold belongs to somebody. The Scavengers either stole it or were transporting it for another party. Now they're dead and we've got it someone's going to be searching for it. Sure, it just might be some legitimate shipment, say from a bank or maybe a big business outfit. But instinct tells me it could well be stolen, and if that's the case you can wager that someone's going to come looking for it . . . the law, outlaws . . . somebody will show up sooner or later. And when that happens, we'll have to fight, run or maybe even turn belly up and hand it over. That what you want?'

Some appeared thoughtful, others did not.

'Let's get it straight, Cole,' said

Courtney Riley, mounting a couple of steps. 'We never cut and run even when we had half of Abe Lincoln's best chasing us through the canebreaks, yet now you want us to ditch this once-in-a-lifetime bonanza on the off chance it could attract a little trouble our way?'

'Right.'

'That's not just dumb,' Riley snapped after a moment. 'It's plain stupid!'

'Every man is entitled to his say, Riley,' Shannon replied calmly. 'And I'll stick by mine.'

Silence.

Jack Quade tugged at his heavy black moustache and frowned deeply. With his crossed feet propped upon the table before him, Kit Quill peered through the V formed by his toes at Shannon, his hawk face reflecting disappointment but lightened by a dawning understanding. Pop Harney appeared sober as he rested a hand upon the gold-packed canvas sack closest to him, while Digger Morgan wore that knotted look which everybody recognized as the Australian's thinking expression.

Gar Brothers hated wrangling and was peering around as if waiting for somebody to explain why in hell everyone was acting so testy, when he felt they should be riding high.

No such uncertainty clouded the handsome features of Courtney Riley.

'You're asking too much, Cole,' he said thinly. 'We've lived rough and dangerous for years and you're asking us to go on doing more of the same even after a fortune drops in our laps.' He shook his head. 'Nobody could be expected to do that, least of all hard-luckers like us.'

'Maybe so,' Shannon conceded. He liked the way the debate was going. Deep down he supposed he agreed they should keep the gold as a spoil of war, but also be smart about how they handled it.

'Well, maybe we can compromise,' he said after a silence. 'This is how I see it. We keep the gold but we sit on it

. . . say for six months until the dust has settled and whoever might be hunting it has quit. If we're still in good shape by then we can talk about loosening the purse-strings and living it up.'

Some scratched their heads while others muttered between themselves. Eventually Jack Quade cleared his throat and spoke up.

'I reckon Cole's thinking the right way, boys. Like he says, the last thing we want to do right now is draw attention. We're strangers here who fought in the war and we need to live quiet for a spell and let the dust settle — '

'Is this an argument or a sermon?' Riley rapped.

'OK,' Quade said amiably. 'I say we stick to our original plan, get us some sorts of jobs maybe, work a spell and keep our noses clean. We could stash the gold and leave it lie for a good spell, then sit down and have the big powwow. That way we are likely to stay alive yet still stay rich. A few months ain't nothing much when you say it quick.'

A long silence.

Then: 'OK, let's have a show of hands,' Pop Harney suggested. 'All for Cole and Jack's notion?'

Only two hands stayed down. Quinn's and Riley's. The young and the hot-headed.

An uneasy silence prevailed until at last Quinn stifled a fake yawn. 'Hell, I'm so much younger than you old duffers, I guess I can afford to wait.' He nodded and winked at Shannon. 'With you, Cole.'

'Six to one,' Pop said. 'So . . . what about it, Court?'

'Look, if I can wait, you can, Riley,' weighed in Digger Morgan. 'I planned to use my cut to send my Libby money to buy herself a ticket from Botany Bay to San Francisco so we can get wedded. And I can tell you I'm about the randiest Aussie in the world right now. So if I can wait I sure as hell reckon you can too. What do you say, boy?'

All eyes were on Riley as seconds ticked the eye-locked silence. There was a yawning feeling that the Brigade was on a knife-edge; that if one member should drop out on a major issue the whole fabric of the band could crumble. For they were seven . . . not six, five . . . or two. They were the Brigade.

'I'm not accepting the vote.'

The wind rustled a sheet of old newsprint along the plankwalk below and an ancient beam creaked overhead. Courtney Riley's words hung in the still, musty air. A challenge had been issued, a line drawn.

No man in Shannon's Brigade had ever contested the vote before.

'Guess you know what this means, Court?' said Shannon.

'Why don't you tell me — big man?'

'It means you're running the risk of getting kicked out of the bunch.'

'The hell it does! All it means is that — '

'You wouldn't be the first to get

marched, mister,' Shannon cut in, his tone cold and hard now. 'The last was Wal Henry. You recall Henry, don't you?'

Riley paled. 'The hell with that — '

'Manning Reach, eighteen sixty-three!' Shannon said inexorably. 'You were a Confederate prisoner after that platoon jumped us at Cemetery Ridge. They were fixing to hang you next morning and I called for a vote to decide if we should risk the whole bunch trying to bust you loose. Henry was the only one to vote against and he was kicked out for it. Then we went and busted you out and it cost us two brave men. Seems I don't recollect you questioning the vote then . . . '

Shannon's words seemed to hang in the air. Riley was pale as he stared from one face to another, each as hard and uncompromising as any other.

For a long moment the young gun's stare was murderous. The next, in a way that was so characteristic, he grinned broadly and clapped a hand to Shannon's shoulder.

'Hell, don't take me serious, Shan. Just testing you out to make sure you're not getting all soft and mushy in your old age, is all. Six months it is. OK, who is buying?'

'Why, I am.' Shannon grinned and extended his hand. 'No hard feelings, Court?'

They shook hands.

'Forgotten, Cole. Hell, everyone knows I can hold my liquor, but I never ever won any prizes for holding a grudge. But now we've settled that, what say we forget about boozing and do some travelling. It's still a ways to this Paiute County we're heading for and, speaking for myself, I'm busting to get a look at this place we're aiming to settle for after all those years. So, what are we waiting for?'

They rode out thirty minutes later and followed the trail deeper into the south-west.

West Texas was vast, the trail seemingly never-ending.

Sunset on their fourth day found

them in the semidesert region of the Sundown Hills. A dry camp, a night disturbed by the distant hooting of wild Indians on some mischief bent, then back into the saddle before first light with old Pop leading them now on a more directly western route.

'Hope you know what you're doing, Pop.' Shannon grinned as they . rode past a solitary stone monument rearing 500 feet into a cloudless sky. 'Looks pretty boondock so far.'

'I tell you it's civilized where we're heading,' came the tetchy response. 'Of course, if you don't have confidence in a man then you can — '

'He's just ribbing you, Pop,' cut in Jack Quade, rocking easily in his double-girthed Texas saddle. 'Funny thing, he did that right through the war and you bit every time.'

Pop scowled, glared from one to the other, then kicked his paint pony ahead, an old man still with a young man's feistiness.

So they pushed on into the unknown

regions of the south-west Texas border country, a bunch of seven slow-moving riders kicking a cloud of butter-coloured dust into an overarching sky.

Rain came overnight and next day they rode through a landscape changing before their eyes. Suddenly the vast dry sweeps were behind them and hills dotted with pine and oak broke the horizon ahead. A great valley opened up gradually before them and they glimpsed rivers and streams in the far distances.

They glanced at one another with foolish pride; they had simply stuck a pin in a map to select their destination, but suddenly they could see it and already it was looking more and more like a lucky choice.

Pop Harney acted smug. He was the only member of the bunch even remotely familiar with this stretch of country and had been convinced from the get-go that Paiute County would suit them all just fine.

They soon moved into the cattle

country. A violent electrical storm overnight forced them to break their next camp and they slogged on to seek the shelter of a deserted high-country ranch house nestled below a stately sagebrush mesa.

It wasn't until the following morning that they discovered they had already reached Paiute County and that the name of their sheltering place was High Tumbleweed Ranch.

Jack Quade was first to notice the rickety old FOR SALE sign wired to the sagging front fence.

It read:

For Sale
HIGH TUMBLEWEED RANCH
See Quentin Kaley, Blue Dog Ranch.

There was a crude drawing of an arrow pointing west to where a pine-clothed hill stood out clearly against an empty sky.

★ ★ ★

Shannon was first abroad early next morning. The weather had blown away and his first impression as he emerged upon the rickety front porch of the old unlocked house was that everything that met his eye appeared even more welcoming than it had the night before.

He took himself for a stroll.

Indicators were that High Tumbleweed had been unoccupied for some time. This puzzled him as it was high and well situated with good grass and ample outbuildings, even if all might be in obvious need of plenty of repair work.

After checking on the horses he pushed open a side gate and walked around the home acres, pausing at the old well which was festooned with cobwebs and totally overgrown by weeds.

Hands thrust into the pockets of his weather jacket, he stood for a time staring thoughtfully back at the house. Run down but solid . . . some ten miles out of town according to Pop . . . close enough for easy access but far enough out as not to be a constant temptation to younger men . . .

He pulled himself up sharply, realizing where his thoughts were leading him. He shook his head. No, he couldn't envision men like Kit, Courtney or even easy-going Gar Brothers being content with this sort of rural life, even if it did already seem to appeal strongly to him.

He had almost reached the first unpainted outbuilding, deep in thought and paying little attention to anything, when a sound caused him to prop and glance sharply towards the trail that went right by the main gate.

He blinked and looked again.

No, he wasn't seeing things, he realized. Sitting a big blood horse by the High Tumbleweed's sagging title gate, and smiling across at him in a way that caused his wrists to tingle, was the best-looking woman he'd sighted since Appomattox. Or maybe ever.

'King,' she smiled, swinging to

ground and acting as though she found nothing unusual in encountering seven gun-toting strangers inhabiting private property. 'Cassie King,' she added, extending a brisk hand to Shannon. 'Welcome to Turkey Track County.'

★　★　★

The kitchen was growing crowded now. Pop and Jack Quade had been abroad fixing coffee on the ancient stove when Shannon came in with the young woman in stylish riding-rig, but once the word circulated they were popping up from everywhere, some still stuffing shirt-tails into pants, Kit Quill and Courtney Riley furiously combing their hair the moment they sighted Cassie King seated upon the ancient table swinging one long leg and tossing auburn curls prettily each time she laughed.

'Well,' she said as the pair stood staring, 'this makes seven by my count, Cole. That's it, I take it?'

'Final tally.' He grinned. 'Er . . . you must understand, Miss King, we just took shelter here overnight. We're not squatters or outlaws or — '

'I can see that,' she said, showing remarkable self-assurance for someone so young. She paused a moment, glancing from one to the other. 'It's a long way from anywhere out here and we don't see many newcomers, what with the war and everything.' Another pause. Then: 'Can I ask if you're passing through or might you be planning to stay on?'

'Haven't decided yet,' Digger Morgan replied. 'But after the war and all we're looking for someplace quiet and what makes some kind of sense, I guess. You could tell us . . . what kind of place is Boiling Fork?'

'Quite agreeable,' she said. Then she smiled cheekily as she slid gracefully from the table. 'Except for my father, that is.'

Seven faces stared at her in puzzlement. She moved for the door, paused.

'Father is the richest man in the county, as you'll quickly discover if you stay on a while. He owns the Monte Cristo copper-mine just outside the town, and has very strong notions about virtually everything . . . including who comes to Boiling Fork and who stays. I'd like to see you men find a home here, if that's what you're looking for. So, my advice is, be polite to my father if you cross paths, but don't let him discourage you. Now I really must be on my way.'

All seven escorted her out to the horse at the hitch rail. Jack Quade untied the animal while Kit Quill gallantly made a cup with his hands which she used as a step to mount.

She glanced around. 'Lovely old place but needs a lot of work . . . and as you can see, it is for sale. Well, thank you for your hospitality, boys, I hope to see you again in town.'

She was swiftly gone, no one moving until she had dropped from sight along the west trail.

'Boys?' Pop said, scratching his head.

'I ain't been called a boy since . . . Hell! Since I was a boy!'

'Sure wouldn't mind being her boy,' Riley said soberly. He looked around at the others. 'You know, I was never that keen about coming to hell and gone out here just to get as far as we could from the war and what comes after, but maybe it wasn't such a bad notion after all?'

'You could be right, man,' put in Kit Quill. He looked dreamy for a moment. 'Hmm . . . Good looker, old man loaded, and she seemed to take to us . . . or to me, leastways. Yeah, Court, I guess you are right. Hey, Pop, you old loser, could be you were smarter than we thought, dragging us to hell and gone out here. What do you say, Cole?'

'I say you jokers clean up here while I go take a good look over this place, then mebbe we should all go take a look at their town . . . and maybe get to meet the man who owns this place,' Shannon replied.

When he swung away to lead them

back to the house it seemed to the others there was a real lightness to his step.

★ ★ ★

He rode slowly across the mesa and began to climb the higher valleys and meadows beyond. The air grew keener up here and a stronger wind blew. Sweeping the unfolding landscape with an expert eye, Shannon made note of the animal pads and stock trails and picked out those meadows where it was most likely the winter snow wouldn't drift, where it would be continually brushed away by the winds to expose the good graze grass underneath.

Feeling like a rancher, thinking like one, he mused; a man could run cattle in this high country but only if he knew what he was doing and wasn't afraid of a little extra work from time to time.

There was always winter grass to be had if you were prepared to go out and find it, and by the time he was pointing

Ulysses's muzzle back towards the headquarters an hour or two later he was already confident he had ear-marked enough winter pastures to accommodate a small to medium sized herd — that was if they were still here when winter came.

He was almost feeling like a genuine rancher again today — like the rancher he'd once been . . .

From a look-out point he stared down upon the patchwork of the headquarters, his gaze drawn to the overgrown head frame of the old well.

They thought him a little loco, he knew. The way he was about the gold, that was. Within days of it falling into their hands he'd begun feeling uneasy about it, at times treating it like something alive and maybe even sinister. He believed that that mysterious shipment of gold carried the stink of bad luck, while at the same time he would be first to concede that that could simply be superstition.

Smoke curled from the ranch-house

chimney and the word 'home' crept unbidden into his thinking as he once again started down.

It was a fine word which had briefly in his loner's life meant a great deal to him . . . and he knew now just how high that word could lift a man, or how low it could bring him.

Home . . .

The word had not bothered Cole Shannon during the war years, for there had been nothing remotely like a home in that time, just one makeshift camp after another, each one as forgettable as the last. But the sight of the ranch house below with smoke drifting from the chimney, along with the possibility that maybe for a time he would be calling this place home, took him back to Virginia where his roots had once gone so deep that nothing on earth could ever have pulled them loose.

They had had to be cut.

The North's army had cut them.

Cut — then buried them.

Something twisted inside him and he

was forced to halt his horse as old emotions came surging to the surface. He fought it, but strength of will wasn't sufficient to hold back the recollection of the spring of 1861 and the last and only time he had known a home and had come home to it, just as men went mad and the world of Cole Shannon caved in . . .

★　★　★

Virginia had appeared calm . . . prosperous and remote from the fledgling war. A thin gentle rain had been falling over the low country as the train covered the last miles to Durantsville. They had laughed at the haste he'd displayed in offloading his horse from the boxcar, and then saddled up and headed directly for home despite the weather. But of course none of them could guess at what he was returning home to . . .

Perhaps they would have understood only too clearly had they seen her as he did an hour later, standing at the gate a full mile from the house beneath a huge black umbrella, waiting for him in the pouring rain.

For a long moment after he swung down they had not spoken. They simply stood there together in the rain, knowing they were different from anyone else, cared more, shared everything and were eternal — even if others might smile or even laugh at such beliefs or notions.

Then she had spoken his name and their lips met.

Her hair smelt like lilacs.

Nobody was crazy enough to believe that the blue army could possibly smash their way through a hundred miles of Confederate-held territory in just a few days, least of all Cole Shannon when he left the following day to finalize his business affairs before returning to take his wife south to the safety of Atlanta.

The Union army rolled over the countryside two nights later. It was a year before Shannon, the Confederate guerrilla leader, could get back to visit her grave . . .

★ ★ ★

'Hey, Cole!'

The swirling memories faded and the pain eased as he came back to the High Tumbleweed Ranch, Texas, 1865.

Shannon blinked then turned his head to see Jack Quade riding across the draw towards him. The big man looked concerned.

'Hey, you all right, Cole?'

'Sure . . . why wouldn't I be?'

'You've been sitting up here an hour. I just figured . . . '

'An hour?' He shook his head. It was hard to believe. 'OK, let's eat dust,' he said, heeling his horse away. 'Er . . . everything OK down below?'

'Sure. When I left Gar was nailing up some loose slats and Pop was cussing weevils in the flour. And I reckon Court and Kit are still mooning about that fine-looking rich gal . . . '

Mention of Cassie King brought a twinge of guilt. There had been no woman for Cole Shannon during the war, or since. Yet he realized with a sense of shock that something about the King girl had slipped under his armour-plating, that there was an aura about her that stayed with a man.

With an act of will he put the rich man's daughter from his mind, didn't realize he was totally silent as they descended to the home acres, when Quade at last spoke up.

'You sure you're OK, man?'

'What? Of course I'm sure. Has anyone told you you fuss like an old woman at times?'

'Only you.' Jack Quade grinned.

Shannon scowled at the man, then laughed. They continued on to the house and the ghosts of his past were gone by the time he stepped down.

4

For and Against

The rider on the black mare was no longer alone on that lonely stretch of trail.

At what exact moment he realized that was unclear, for he was a man travelling fast with long miles behind and with still a good sweep of country remaining ahead before he would sight his destination.

Thinking back on it now as the good horse maintained a brisk clip, the horseman realized his instincts had been subtly warning him that something was not exactly as it should be for quite a spell now.

It could happen like that, he knew, particularly when a man was travelling in lonesome, nothing kind of country such as this windy stretch of Texas. A man's instincts sharpened at such times, and he liked to believe he had better instincts than just about anyone.

He hipped around in the saddle.

Nothing.

He grinned. Another man might brush his concerns aside at this point and tell himself he was imagining things. Not him. Not Lucky Ned Pepper. He had more respect for his instincts than most people he knew. They had saved his life more than once and might do so again today — depending on who might be trailing him, and why.

Another mile drifted by.

This time when he turned again his saturnine features quirked with self-congratulation. For there they were in plain sight some a couple miles back now. Two of them slamming along the trail, just black dots of motion at first but quickly swelling to form into the shapes of horsemen in the dusk light.

He believed they were riding like men who had maybe picked up a scent.

He was peeved, yet still managed a trademark chuckle as he put pressure upon the horse's withers with his knees and gigged it into a faster lope.

He reminded himself he really didn't have time for joining in whatever kind of deviltry these Lone Star Staters might be hatching. He would prefer to try and shake them before the time he reached the way station at Hawk Hollow. But if he failed to do so, then . . .

Another grin. He smiled much more than usual these days. With good reason. He'd struck big money at the end of a period of tough times, what with his having been chased clear across the Staked Plains by those lousy Texas Rangers and all.

On the bright side, he had a huge cache waiting for him ahead, and if he had at last given the manhunters the shake he would just as soon avoid any further trouble right here and now.

Yet it was a fact of life that Lucky Ned Pepper would only ever run just so far. A man had his pride.

It was black as a lawman's soul by the time he raised Los Ydros. A tiny outpost in the heartland of noplace, Los Ydros catered for the weary traveller. He was well into his second brandy and half-way through his half-raw steak when the batwings creaked open and in they came.

He knew it had to be his tail just by the way they cut their eyes this way and that around the saloon, not focusing until they spotted him.

He sighed and set down knife and fork. Why did they do it? Whether they were lawmen, bounty hunters or just a pair of hicks with big ideas — didn't they ever learn how to tell the difference between badmen it was safe to go chasing after, and the other kind? His kind, in particular.

For himself, he had always had a natural instinct as to what man to take after, and whom to leave strictly alone. But then, he had always been smarter than most.

They were wary before approaching. Pros, he could tell. Likely they'd expected him to have his bunch with him. He mostly did. In truth, he was overdue to link up with his regular gang half a day's ride from here before pushing on to his ultimate destination where even more guns would be waiting. Now . . . what was the name of that second destination? Cracker Creek? Didn't sound like much, he would admit. But what was in a name? There were men waiting for him there, watching over his fortune in yellow gold, the rewards of his biggest and boldest job ever.

His line of thought broke off as he glanced up. At last the John Laws had decided he was here alone, and were starting across the room.

Sons of bitches.

He leaned back then rose smoothly, a trim-bodied man with shoulder-length hair and compelling eyes of china blue. And two big guns whose walnut handles reflected the light as he brushed back the panels of his coat back to hook behind them.

The pair propped. The big one sported a fat moustache and plainly liked the sound of his own deep voice.

'You are the gentleman known as Edward Clancy Pepper, right?'

'Why, yes, you've got me fitted right, stranger. Old Lucky Ned in the flesh. And who might you be, if it ain't a rude question?'

The two had spread out, hands close to guns, eyes transmitting the clear warning: go for your guns and you are dead meat, Pepper!

'I'm carrying a sheriff's warrant authorizing the capture or killing of the outlaw Edward Clancy Pepper, known as Lucky Ned who — '

But Lucky Ned had heard more than enough by this, and the big man was still banging on when his twin guns leapt from leather like live things to spew out twin jets of raging gunflame with a roar to shake the building to its foundations. Struck hard and fatally at point-blank range the two figures in dusty brown instantly began buckling, twisting and jerking violently like Punch and Judy figurines gone loco, with great gouts of crimson spurting from their bodies as they crashed blindly into each other before crashing to the floor side by side.

The gunsmoke was still drifting thickly when the killer light-footed his way through the batwings, sprang into the saddle, and dug spurs.

Eye-witnesses claimed later they heard him laughing as he galloped from that town.

★   ★   ★

'Well, here he comes at last,' Riley said, glancing through the dusty kitchen window. 'Can someone tell me why anybody would want to get up at false dawn and spend two hours wandering all over a nowhere dump like this on his lonesome? You know, boys, maybe all those close calls we had and the good pards we lost back there have finally got him? Could he be cracking up?'

There was no telling if Courtney Riley was jesting or not. He was a complex man who tended to tangle with Shannon from time to time, and had already done so here at High Tumbleweed Ranch.

Shannon had shown immediate interest in the battered FOR SALE sign inside the old gates, had noted that the property's agent could be located at a neighbouring ranch further down the trail.

Riley had wanted to head straight on into the town but for some reason Shannon had insisted they camp here overnight, a mighty strange decision to Riley's way of thinking.

The door swung open and Shannon came in looking thoughtful. Seated around the big old table, five veterans turned to stare, while Pop Harney at the range went right on fixing breakfast.

'So?' Gar Brothers said. 'What?'

'What?' Shannon echoed, still distant.

Brothers spread big hands. 'You've been up half the night like a vampire. It ain't natural after the miles we've been putting in. So, I'll ask you again. What?'

'I like it — that's what.'

Pop dropped his skillet and Courtney Riley swore. 'I knew it!' the young gun said accusingly. 'Damnit, I sensed it when we rode in. That dumb-ass For Sale sign did it. You looked around, could suddenly see us all settling down to playing cowboys and living off the fat of the land, and so you went and — '

'Take it easy,' Shannon cut in, accepting a steaming mug of joe from Pop. 'Sure, I like the look of the place, and maybe I feel it could be a smart notion for us to maybe put down roots for a spell . . . but like I say, just a notion.' He paused a moment then flashed his rare smile. 'Anyway, no big hurry.' He dipped his fingers into his breast pocket and drew forth a sheet of folded paper. He tapped it with his

78

fingertip. 'On account we've got it leased for a month.'

For a long moment the big old room was totally silent. Then everybody began talking at once, while Shannon still grinned. He could not explain what had prompted him to ride five miles to visit the land agent named on the FOR SALE board. But he'd liked Quentin Kaley, the rancher-cum-agent seemed to take to him, so they'd done a small deal. Tenancy of High Tumbleweed Ranch for one month while Shannon and his pards got things sorted out. What harm in that?

Of course, he had anticipated opposition might be strong but that didn't prove to be the case. Sure, Riley was irked and Quill did some cursing as the debate continued. But men like Quade, Harney and Morgan didn't appear too negative.

Shannon wondered if it would change anything if they had opposed what he'd done. And pausing to examine that challenging thought, he quickly realized what lay behind his decision.

Exhaustion. Simple really.

He was understanding that he'd led the brigade for too long, had seen too many men under his command lowered into the ground. The survivors had looked to him to lead them after Appomattox, and they had ended up here at the tip-end of Texas where they knew nobody and nobody knew them. He didn't know if the ranch was worth a damn, or if all or none of them really wanted to take up ranching.

But it was a place a man might get to rest up, do some healing and get his bearings then eventually make an informed decision on what they could all agree upon regarding the future for Shannon's Brigade.

He silenced them eventually and called for a vote. He'd feared it might run as high as six to one against. But that proved not to be the case.

Within minutes it was clear that Digger, Quade and Pop were prepared to go along with his decision. Kit Quill then claimed he couldn't be bothered wrangling and said he'd go with a majority vote.

That still left Riley and Brothers opposed, and at the end of an at times heated half hour, that remained the case.

It would be midday before an agreement would be reached to go visit the town. Everyone realized they needed to see just what sort of town Boiling Fork might be before making any decision about staying on. Even more important was the opportunity to put their feet up, have a few drinks and genuinely unwind.

Shannon's response was cool but inside he felt he'd already won.

Before quitting the High Tumbleweed the seven crossed the ranch yard where they lowered a heavy leather satchel down the disused well, which they then covered with the same rubble and detritus that had filled it before.

He hoped this would prove a smart

move for more reasons than one. Shannon wanted them to consider his proposal calmly and quietly without the gold sitting up staring at them and maybe clouding their brains.

It was an assorted mixture of smiles, scowls, sullen silences and garrulous debate that characterized the Brigade as they covered the ten-mile trail to the valley and the mining town of Boiling Fork, where the first stop-off was the Nugget saloon.

★ ★ ★

'Passing through or staying on, gents?'

The bartender with the huge waxed moustaches was curious yet didn't appear nosy.

'Resting up some up at High Tumbleweed while we get our bearings,' Brothers supplied.

Drinkers overheard and nodded to one another. Sounded reasonable, they supposed. There were any number of folks on the move all over after the peace in these uncertain post-war days.

Yet some still appeared a little uneasy about all the guns. The 'Shannon outfit', as the barkeep dubbed them following introductions all appeared to favour low-slung sixshooters and gave a strong impression that they were capable of using them.

Yet within a couple of hours their novelty had worn off. Then the afternoon shift ended at the Monte Cristo Mine and the newcomers merged in with the crowd after a dozen sweating and rough-garbed Cousin Jacks stomped in hollering for one thing only — beer, and keep it coming.

So far so good, mused Shannon as a brassy percentage girl topped up his glass. And when the cocky Riley strolled across to the girl, chucked her under the chin and flashed her his best smile, he told himself he could at last allow himself to relax fully.

And wondered: how long since he had felt that way? The answer, of course, was: too long. So he ordered another and had it in his hand when trouble shouldered its way through the batwing doors.

The security guards from the mine didn't mince words. A load of ore was missing from the day's production and the Henderson work party were the prime suspects.

There was something inevitable and primitive about the brawl that erupted almost immediately, and Shannon soon found himself almost enjoying the spectacle from half-way up the stairs, while Kit Quill and Pop Harney were urging the fighters on below.

It was totally violent while it lasted but, to his war-jaded eyes, appeared almost harmless. The worst likely to come out of the dust-up would be a broken nose or snapped tooth. Six weeks earlier, he'd been gunning down men wearing Abe Lincoln blue like fish in a barrel from behind a chattering Gatling gun. This was kid stuff by comparison.

By the time it was over and saloon

hands were cleaning up, the mood of the seven was relaxed and easy and some even seemed to be getting comfortable in their new surroundings.

Shannon hoped that that would continue to be the case. He hadn't even confided to Jack Quade yet that he'd made up his mind that, no matter how many of the seven might eventually elect to move on, he would be staying put in Paiute County.

This veteran was 'done wandering'.

★　★　★

Shannon lay on an ancient canvas cot in the storeroom of the High Tumbleweed ranch house stretching his legs beneath the worn blanket. It was still dark but he knew it was close to morning.

He stared up at the ceiling and blinked away the last dregs of sleep . . . and the dream.

The dream was always the same; wave after wave of howling cavalrymen in Yankee blue thundering towards the bunch, never drawing closer and never falling back. Until somehow he'd managed to jolt himself awake.

Pop Harney, a veteran of other, older wars, had assured him the dream would leave him in time. He just must be patient, was all.

He grinned as he swung his feet to the floor and reached for hat and boots. Their third day at the Tumbleweed, yet he was still waking too early, as though he couldn't wait to be up and about.

His hangover made itself felt when he stood to pull on his pants. They had packed bottled supplies back from town and had made heavy inroads since while debating — would they stay or would they go? It was a debate Shannon was refusing to be drawn into right now, yet he suspected all knew where he stood. Just last night, Brothers had accused him of being 'mule-stubborn and pig-headed', yet later Pop had confided that he seen 'worse places to hang your hat' than High Tumbleweed Ranch.

The morning was crisp and cool with just a hint of autumn in the air as he drew on a leather jacket and moved quietly through to the kitchen where he sluiced cold water over his face from the half-barrel in the corner by the clanky old stove.

He was tempted to brew coffee but decided against it. He would likely raise a clatter getting the range fired up. In any case, now he was dressed he was eager to get outside.

Fitting his hat to his head he went out and stood on the front porch. All around, the world lay hushed, the land seeming to breathe softly in that gentle hour between night and day. To the south there was a gap in the cloud and a few brave stars were visible through the rain.

He inhaled the clean chill air and his mouth quirked at the corners. This was the time of day he liked best. There was no sin in the early morning, no ugliness

— and no muttering cannon. Even during the war years he had enjoyed early mornings alone, planning the day's schedule, carrying the burden of leadership with apparent ease.

He crossed to the stables where he fed Ulysses from a bucket then set about saddling the animal with the skill of long practice.

The horse was frisky in the early morning and was well-rested now — maybe for the first time in its life. Once clear of the headquarters Shannon gave him his head. They followed the trace of the south meadow at the lope, then swung half-right at the lightning-split cottonwood and made towards the southern boundary.

Shannon tugged his tin of cigars from the jacket pocket and set one alight one-handed with the skill of long practice. He was inhaling deeply in the early daylight when something caught his eye from the slope of the hill ahead.

A fresh shower drew a metallic curtain briefly across the strengthening light as he cut across the flat and began to climb. The ground was soggy up here but Ulysses was sure-footed and safe.

Eventually he reined in to find himself staring down at the single line of hoof tracks that came in from the west, the direction of the distant valley town, crossed the slope at an angle before disappearing into the timberline to the south.

The sign was fresh and the animal that left it wore shoes with square-headed nails. None of their mounts was shod with nails that shape.

But the rich man's daughter rode a horse that did!

Mere minutes earlier, Shannon had been musing on weighty matters concerning the past, the gold, their immediate future here. But this threw his thoughts into confusion, and staring in the direction the horse had gone he was trying to find some reason to justify that handsome young woman riding up here again as she plainly had done in the early hours.

It didn't figure.

All he knew was that for some reason he found it exciting that she had been out here in the cold darkness watching the spread.

Then in the same moment, he felt a chill. For if Cassie King could come that close without anybody being aware of it, it meant that others could do so also.

He turned his head to stare at the barely visible old well, thinking of the treasure and was forced to reflect again on the old adage that nothing on earth attracts trouble like the scent, the rumour or simply the vaguest hint of yellow gold.

He knew then, as he believed he'd likely known all along, that the bunch could never afford to relax while ever the gold was part of their lives. And turning Ulysses's head for the house, he resolved to post a look-out every night. Just in case.

★　★　★

The noon sun hung over the ghost town, its clean yellow light flooding the decaying buildings aged by wind and weather, the warped doors and fading signs that hung above the empty street.

The town was still, the hollow rooms without sound.

Far up the street, beyond the reservoir, a road-runner raced into view, teetered briefly atop a boulder, then was gone.

Cassie King sat her horse upon the bluff above the old trail and gazed down upon the town. After a minute or two she turned her head to let her eyes play over the jumble of half-collapsed buildings as if searching for signs of life.

She was. But today, unlike other days when she visited the Warcloud ruins, she was also keeping one eye apprehensively open for any sign of her father.

The richest man in the south-western county had ordered his headstrong daughter to cease visiting the crumbling ghoster. He could never understand why she insisted on doing so, any more than he could or would try to comprehend why she did so many of those other things which annoyed him, that she did continually.

He was thinking in terms of such weird behaviour as her operating a soup-kitchen in Boiling Fork, visiting the sick or assisting Doc Watson in patching up men injured in his Monte Cristo Mine — or, worse, visiting their families.

He admired his daughter's independence and spirit but not when they conflicted with his notion of how a respectable young woman should behave.

After some time, the girl kneed her mount forward and allowed it pick its own trail down. The day was heating up and the horse sweated from the journey back from the Tumbleweed — yet another place she had been warned to avoid.

She was thinking of those new men there as the horse carried her along the echoing main street. She hoped the new-comers might elect to stay on at the old place.

Boiling Fork needed new blood, she believed, and an infusion of seven likely-looking males couldn't do the town anything but good, to her way of thinking.

The hoofbeats echoed hollowly against the sagging and faded falsefronts on either side. Though many of the side streets of the ghoster were overgrown with sage and maguey, the main stem was clear due to the regular traffic that passed through here from Boiling Fork to the tin-mining settlement of Tarpot to the south.

Approaching the hotel, Cassie rested her hand upon the butt of the .32 six-shot protruding from her boot-top holster.

The weapon was no ornament. The young woman shot as expertly as she rode, and even though daring and even reckless in the eyes of some, she rarely took foolish chances.

The deadly little weapon was her insurance should she encounter rattlers, either the kind that crawled or those that walked on two legs.

But today Warcloud's crooked main stem appeared empty but for two motionless lizards which watched the intruder with bright jewelled eyes from the porch of the old bakery house. Eventually she reined in and stepped down to hitch the chestnut at the tie rack before the saloon where she stood gazing about her, savouring the silence and air of mystery and decay she found so intriguing.

But so far, still no sign of those whom she had come to visit.

She wandered about for an hour or more without sighting any sign of those she thought of as 'her people'. Then she paused as she caught sight of distant horsemen on the town trail to the south.

She grimaced when she was able to identify the riders. Her father was one of them. Momentarily she considered mounting up and taking a back trail home to Boiling Fork instead of waiting for her father to show. Then she shook her head stubbornly.

No, that would be showing weakness.

Her father considered her stubborn and single-minded to a fault. It was possible she was both. But she would never change. To have done so would be to give Barlow King encouragement to believe she could yet be 'saved' from her obstinate nature, as he termed it.

She was back in the saddle and riding innocently along the main stem some time later when the horsemen swung into sight at the southern end of the street. Her father appeared first followed by Gordy Miller, the mine foreman, and Jet Brogan, Barlow King's hatched-faced bodyguard, riding side by side.

Tall, square-shouldered and formidable astride his blood-red stallion, Barlow King stiffened upon seeing his daughter, then clamped black brows down tight as he kicked ahead to be first to reach her side.

'And just what in the name of all that's holy do you think you are doing to hell and gone out here again, missy?' he barked. He was a man accustomed to yelling, due partly to a hearing defect but largely on account of a temperament which some regarded as poisonous. His eyes raked the desolate street suspiciously. 'Alone!'

'Your blood pressure, Father,' Cassie said quietly. 'Remember what Doc Watson said?'

'The hell with my blood pressure and that blood-and-bowels medical fraud to boot! Damnation, girl, isn't it enough that I had to ride thirty miles to talk with a cretin who wouldn't know a favourable business opportunity from a hole in his underdrawers . . . I'm not even home before I find you out wandering and disobeying my specific orders — '

'I take it then that Cy Webb turned down your offer on his smelter then, Father?' the girl cut in adroitly.

King's bull jaw sagged. He stared at his daughter bleakly, a big man running a little to flab but still hard, still running his own show.

'That's so,' he eventually conceded. 'Damn fool, no wonder he has to slog fourteen hours a day to keep his family fed — Just a damn minute! You're not getting me off the track that easily, Miss Clever.'

He paused in puzzlement. 'Wait . . . just what the hell are you doing to hell and gone out here anyway?'

'Yeah . . . what?' Brogan cut in.

She flicked the hard man a cold glance. Cassie King didn't get along with Jet Brogan. Eventually her dislike had gotten through to the man so that they now shared a hostile relationship.

King plucked a flask from his hip-pocket and tipped it to his lips. Doc Watson had warned the miner concerning his whiskey consumption in relationship to his blood pressure, but King was a man more at home giving orders than taking them.

'Come on, madam, we can talk as we travel,' he growled. 'This place always gave me the creeps.'

They got under way, but Cassie was

quick to mount a distraction before King could get started on her again.

'I visited High Tumbleweed earlier, Father. Susie needed the exercise, and I was also curious to see if the new people were still there.'

'New people?' King grumped. 'Does that mean Quentin Kaley has leased that white elephant of his at last?'

'Abe has been able to graze stock up there on and off for almost a year, so it can't be all that bad,' Cassie replied. She paused a moment, then added: 'That bunch of nice-looking gentlemen who came to town appear to have put up there overnight again . . . so I think they must be interested in the place . . .'

'Nice-looking, you say?' King's stare was suspicious. He knew his daughter was considered highly attractive by the menfolk and firmly intended that she would make a wonderful match-up with her wealthy suitor, and the sooner the better. 'How many of these bums did you say there are?'

'Seven.'

King hunched his shoulders. 'Seven bums on High Tumbleweed? Just what the county needs — like hell! And . . . and you've been up there?'

He turned to his bodyguard. 'You hear that, Brogan?'

'Sure did, boss man.'

'So, what do you make of it?'

'Well, what with all kinds of bums and trash wandering the countryside since the peace, Mr King . . . I guess I just plain didn't think about them at all.'

'Well, you and I think differently, mister.' Barlow King twisted in the saddle to gaze up at the high slopes to the north-east. He came to a decision. 'Miller, you ride in with Cassie. Brogan, you and I are going on ahead to alert the sheriff about this.'

'The sheriff, Father . . . ?' Cassie began, but got no further as the two men kicked their horses and took off at a swift lope. She was sober as she watched the pair ride out of sight before turning to the rider at her side.

'Gordy, why is he so angry?'

'Well, you know your pa, missy, he's a mighty suspicious feller at the best of times. But I reckon this time he might have reason. I mean, a whole bunch of gun-hung strangers talking about maybe settling in could mean new trouble for the town, maybe even for Mr King personal. Feller in the boss's position has always gotta be wary both for himself and his town.'

'But . . . but Boiling Fork needs new blood, new ideas, Gordy. And some of them appear quite impressive at first meeting — '

'They still could be owl hoot, Miss Cassie. Or mebbe even they might be gun muscle brought in by the miners. You know how they keep griping about low wages and dangerous conditions. Who knows, they could be planning to stage a take-over or something like?'

Cassie started to shake her head, then stopped. Shannon most assuredly did not fit the gunman or outlaw mould to her way of thinking. But when she concentrated on some of his companions, she no longer felt so certain. One or two had looked at least slightly dangerous, particularly that sleek young man called Riley . . .

Cassie King was mostly silent all the way home after that. It would be just her luck she told herself a little bitterly, and with just a touch of a spoiled girl's petulance, that the first really interesting man she had encountered in ages, Cole Shannon, should turn out to be some kind of outlaw.

It simply wasn't fair!

*   *   *

Over the years the Brigade had seen hard times and made many a tough decision. They'd wrangled in the dugouts along the Atlantic coast and occasionally almost come to blows behind enemy lines once or twice in Virginia.

Even so, the wrangle building towards

a climax at midnight that night was plainly as heated as any they'd had before, and after several hours of it Cole Shannon found himself forced to pull rank.

'All right, all goddamn right!' he announced, moving to stand before the empty fireplace in the ranch house's front room. 'If we can't get unanimity we'll accept majority vote!'

Six faces stared at him. Majority vote had only been called twice in the Brigade's history. And both those occasions had been under war-time conditions. It didn't seem right to have to resort to that extreme here in old Texas in peacetime, but that was plainly how strong the for-and-against opinions went.

A couple began to object but Shannon silenced them with a curt gesture.

'No, we've talked it out. This is the only way it can be settled. OK, show of hands. All in favour of keeping the gold stashed and pooling our resources to buy up this place and work it for a trial six months, then have us another meeting — how do you vote?'

Four hands went up immediately, eventually followed by a fifth, although even then easy-going Gar Brothers didn't appear convinced he was making the right choice.

'Five for, two against.' Cole nodded. 'So, four wins. Too bad, Court and Kit.'

'Just a minute!' Courtney Riley had argued long and eloquently against the decision to support the leader's choice. He looked pale and angry now, but was not given the opportunity to take it further as Cole spoke over him.

'Debate over!' he stated. 'Tomorrow afternoon we ride to town and lodge our bid.' He paused a moment before adding: 'Any man who still opposes the decision can demand his cut of the gold . . . and quit. That's how we've always operated and always will while ever the Brigade survives.'

He turned to quit the room, paused.

'I'll be on the gallery if anybody wants to discuss this further.' His eyes scanned every face. 'I hope I don't see anybody, but if I do, well, it'll hurt the bunch, but it will survive. Four years of war couldn't bring us down, so nothing I've seen here in this county is going to change that.'

The first ten minutes that he spent on the rickety old front porch with a cigarette seemed as long as he had ever experienced, a painful reminder of just how much the bunch meant to him. Nobody showed.

Another ten and Cole Shannon found himself unable to stop grinning with relief as he stepped down and strolled across the moon-washed ranch yard.

Pausing to look up at the sky, he was thinking this had to be one of the best moments ever.

The Brigade had survived!

5

Hellion Breed

Navajo Joe brushed sensitive fingertips across an innocent-looking slab of bluestone, then put pursed lips close to the rock and softly blew. A little cloud of dust rose and quickly fell. The Indian rolled his eyes at the testy figure sitting his saddle a short distance away.

'What you see?' he asked with seeming innocence. In reality he was up to his old tricks of playing games on others, particularly the Invaders — or white men. In this instance he had a strong notion where to look for the tracks his client so desperately wanted him to find, but because of his capricious nature, he meant to string it out, even try to make his current employer look a little foolish before giving him what he was being paid for.

That was a mistake.

'Good question,' the client answered. 'Well, if you want me to be honest, I'd say what I'm mainly seeing is a redskin without the brains of a gopher who could get splattered all over this here freaking basin in about five seconds if he don't quit playing games and comes up with sign.'

By way of emphasis, Lucky Ned Pepper whipped out a .45 faster than the eye could follow. A crashing report, and the slab of blue stone disintegrated, peppering the tracker's bronzed face with fragments.

'Catch on?' he said.

By this the tracker had sprung erect to massage his face, and stared incredulously at the blood streaking his fingers. A man revered in many circles for his great skills as sign-reader, Navajo Joe's big-nosed face showed murderous rage, but only for a moment. The hot glare in the man's eye faded totally as the soft metallic click of the still-smoking gun being cocked reached his sound-dulled senses.

'OK . . . all right,' he panted, realizing his huge error of judgement. 'Joe look . . . and Joe find.'

'Joe had better.'

There was some sniggering from the five sitting their saddles a short distance away as the tracker began covering ground in quick jerky steps, hindquarters in the air and intent face lowered comically close to the ground.

Beaudine O'Toole didn't join in the amusement. That outlaw had ridden with Lucky Ned before and knew just how lethally irrational he could be when the wind might blow from the wrong direction, or when, as in this case, someone might have the brass-bound nerve to steal from him.

It had been a brutal blow for Lucky Ned to arrive late for the rendezvous at Cracker Creek only to find four recently-dug shallow graves and ten grand in gold missing.

The proceeds of a daring scam and robbery staged right under the noses of the military in Georgia, the gold had been taken west on his instructions by whatever low-life outlaw recruits Lucky Ned was able to muster at short notice. The band made it to well clear of the danger zones only to wind up shot to doll-rags at the rendezvous by . . . who could tell?

Pepper was too much the professional to waste time bemoaning his misfortune. He always knew where the talent was to be found, and he'd had the cocky yet highly skilled Navajo Joe back at the creek with him within twenty-four hours.

This man-hunter was costing him big money. Ned expected that. But what he didn't expect — and would never tolerate — was somebody not paying him due respect.

'My watch is ticking, wigwam!' he called after lighting a cheroot. 'You've got . . . ' He paused to drag out a fob watch. 'Ahh . . . another five minutes. No, damnit, make that four. You lose one minute for acting the smart-ass.'

The big-nosed Navajo thought he was joking. But only for a moment. Years of dangerous living had educated the man, making him just as adept at reading character as following sign.

The moment he realized that Pepper might haul one of those flash pistols and cut him down should he fail to treat both him and his job with due seriousness, Joe became a changed man.

He quit playing to the gallery and concentrated with all he had.

From here on in he would play it straight.

He had not done that totally while following the old and fading sign into the south-west from Cracker Creek over two long days. Sure, he'd been doing the job professionally and successfully but without actually informing Pepper of his progress. Until now. In moments he had brought the killer fully up to date on what he knew, guessed and predicted concerning their quarry. He insisted he now knew exactly where to look for more sign, and did so promptly at the run, criss-crossing the sandy depression on skinny big-footed legs with nothing escaping his eyes until he spotted what he was searching for.

It was merely a faint depression in soft earth close to a protecting boulder, a faint six inches long and a half-inch deep. But very readable to the eye of a professional.

'Cannon wagon go by here!' he announced with confidence.

Lucky Ned heeled his horse across and reined in. He smiled slowly when he made out the wheelmark in the earth. He even smiled at his tracker now, although it didn't reach his eyes.

'You do good work, boy. See how easy it is when you put your mind to it? OK, so which way were they heading when they came through here?'

Navajo Joe stood militarily upright, raised his right arm with fingers extended to point at the sky, then slowly but confidently brought the arm down to the horizontal where he locked it steady with stiffened fingers now pointing west by south-west.

Lucky Ned signalled to his bunch and they followed Navajo Joe at a jingling walk-trot.

The five riding with Pepper were among the most lethal men in Texas. They went a long way back with the outlaw who might well have rated that 'most lethal' tag. Riding with Ned in the past, they had been both rich and poor, but most often rich. They were to be paid in gold coin if they tracked down his treasure.

None of the outlaws glanced back the way they'd come from Cracker Creek as they set off on the tracker's heels. There was no need. And even if they had done so it was unlikely they'd have sighted anything. For if there was one skill upon which the large slow-moving man who had been trailing them over the vast miles from Cracker Creek prided himself at being more expert than another, it was in not drawing attention to himself.

US Treasury Agent Haig Marlowe was lethal with a long rifle, yet did not see himself as either hero or fighter. But when it came to hunting down fortunes of gold, currency or other valuables which criminals might plunder from Uncle Sam from time to time, this outsized and lethal professional was in a class all his own.

★　★　★

'Yeeehahh!' yelled Gar Brothers, waving his sombrero over his head. 'Saturday night in the big city! Oh, how long, oh Lord, how long?'

It was a boomingly boisterous shout that rolled down Main and drew some attention from the early evening crowds along the plankwalks. But the overall effect was disappointing, at least from Brothers's point of view. For the fact was, Boiling Fork was no longer anything like the cheerful, yeah-saying kind of Texan town that it might have been one or two years earlier.

There were a number of reasons for this. Early on, large profits had been made from the copper gouged out of the Monte Cristo, but these had gone exclusively to King's company while the men doing all the work failed even to rate a raise. In recent times the rich seams had begun to fail alarmingly out at the mine situated five miles west of town, and meagre wage-packets had shrunk by the month.

A second exploratory shaft sunk a mile south of the mine had shown some promise at first, but work there was at a standstill because of King's difficulty in securing investment capital, which once had been readily available.

The result of this had been a marked increase in owner-worker hostility, with poverty grinding away at the latter class while Barlow King continued to throw glittering dinners for influential friends and potential investors — while boasting that his daughter would soon be announcing her betrothal to Pauite

County's most eligible and wealthy bachelor.

Small wonder a man could get into a fight most anytime in Boiling Fork without half trying these testing days. But it was far more difficult to draw a laugh, or a positive response to an exuberant yell, as Gar Brothers was finding out.

'What's the name of this place, did you say?' He scowled. 'Tombstone? Or was it Deadwood?'

'You're an hour too early is all.' Shannon grinned, riding a horse-length ahead. He gestured. 'See, everyone's just getting home from work. They don't want woolly-headed wranglers hollering at them when they're all dry and tuckered out. And that would go double for strangers, I'd figure.'

'Who asked you, Cole?' The big man grinned. 'I don't recall — ' He broke off mid-sentence and twisted in the saddle to follow the progress of a pretty-eyed blonde swinging her hips down the sidewalk by the saloon. 'Whooee! Now what was I saying? I plumb forget. Maybe I'm losing my mind.'

The banter continued as they approached the central block. It sounded good to Shannon's ears. There had been tension around the spread concerning the gold, but this had seemed to be on the wane during the ride in.

'Sheesh! Who kicked the trash can over?'

The derisive yell caused seven heads to turn. A bunch of laid-off workers in miners' Levis were slouched untidily across the front porch of an unpainted saloon, glaring at them passing by. Kit Quill laughed and blew them a kiss. An angry Cousin Jack started down the steps but a companion hooked him under the armpit and hauled him back with a warning shake of the head. The man's lips moved and he might have said: 'Guntippers!'

Riding at Shannon's side, Digger Morgan shouted something offensive but failed to draw a response.

The bunch was not usually this

aggressive, but the town had proved unfriendly and even half-way hostile towards them before, and it was second nature for them to react in kind.

★   ★   ★

Shannon was studying the awning sign that said Duel Street. Morgan didn't know it, but Shannon did. It was where Cassie King lived with her father, and he could see the mansion lights faintly through the dusk now. Shannon was feeling good for some reason as they turned in at the livery where stable-boys emerged to take charge of the horses.

Yet he still remained watchful as they headed for the saloon, always their first port of call. For this was a troubled and turbulent town where citizens were anything but sure why seven formidable strangers would want to show up out of nowhere and take a lease on a run-down cattle spread. The bunch had heard they were anything but popular with both the local sheriff and Barlow King, and could identify plenty more who didn't seem to cotton to their style for one reason or another.

This bothered them not at all. They would survive easily enough. Even so, Shannon still delayed them at the saloon's front doors gallery to issue a last low-key warning against raising hell before leading them inside.

A bearded man on King's payroll watched them disappear inside, then hurried up Duel Street for the mansion.

★ ★ ★

'I've heard this all before, Hinch,' King snapped, tapping his pipestem on the desk blotter. 'Gripe, gripe, gripe! Is that what they pay you to do? Why don't you start acting like a real workers' rep and start persuading them to lift their work rate? Something positive, for a change.'

'If you wanna know the truth, Mr King, the workers are taking less and less notice of me as time goes by — '

'Figures,' sneered Jet Brogan, standing half in shadows in back of the big desk.

'I'll handle this,' King snapped. He leaned forward. 'All right, Hinch, you've done complaining about everything under the sun. If that's all you've got you might as well get going. I'm late for supper.'

The rawboned miners' rep got to his feet, clutching his hat in his hands.

'There's one more thing, Mr King. You've cut wages and upped the workload one time too many, and they just ain't going to take it any long — '

'Look, you moron!' King said loudly, getting up. 'I've told you before and I'll tell you again. The seams are playing out, production is way down and I'm currently running at a loss. And you and your clock-watchers are just too dumb to believe it. Well, if — '

King broke off as a man appeared in the doorway. 'What is it, damnit?'

'Just come from the saloon, Mr King.

118

Er . . . some fellers just rode in . . . '

'All right.' King came round the desk. 'Fill in the blank spaces yourself, Hinch. Tell them if they don't like conditions they can quit.'

'They can't do that, Mr King, not with all the back wages you owe them and all — ' the man began. But Brogan moved swiftly to seize him by the arm and proceeded to bundle him roughly from the room.

King beckoned the new arrival closer. 'Yeah, Strat, what is it?'

The man from the Nugget moved into the light. 'Them geezers just showed up, Mr King. You know? That outfit from the High Tumbleweed.'

'How many?' King's tone was sharp.

'All of 'em, Mr King. Seven.'

'Including this man Shannon?'

The fellow nodded and King waved him out before resuming his chair.

'As if a man hasn't enough troubles,' he growled, torching a cigar into life. He coughed and cursed. 'Seams cutting out, explorations not showing anything yet, daughter's misbehaving . . . and now she's making eyes at this — what the hell is his name again?'

'Shannon,' supplied Brogan as he returned.

'And what have we been able to find out about Mr Shannon?' King asked with an edge to his voice.

'Very little — '

'You mean nothing?'

'Guess that's what I do mean, boss.'

King threw his weight back in the big padded chair and blew smoke at the ceiling. Then he swivelled to stare at the framed picture above the cold fireplace which showed a handsome young man, immaculately tailored and fairly oozing fine breeding.

'Educated, in love with her, family loaded . . . ' he muttered like a man thinking out loud. 'His father could finance my new shaft for me and not even notice it . . . could save me, the Cristo and her, for that matter. It's all up for grabs. But what does Miss Difficult do? Claps her eyes on some bum from Bumsville, and next thing she's telling this finest catch in the county — a man who's got everything and especially money — she is too busy to see him at the weekend. Tell me, Brogan, does that make any kind of sense to you?'

The bodyguard's response was predictable.

'No, it don't, boss. Er . . . do you want me to round up some of the boys and maybe — '

'Damnit, don't you ever learn?' King overrode him roughly. 'I've only had one look at that bunch but that was more than enough to send me a big warning message. So maybe they are bums. They could be owl hoot, draft-dodgers from the war, Democrat voters or wandering gypsies. Could be! But one thing they sure enough are, mister — no maybe about it — is dangerous. I smell it and feel it and I'm never wrong about things like that, can't afford to be. My hunch is that they're vets of some kind, but two or three of them at least sure shape up as the fighting kind. And you want to rough them up! When are you going to stop acting like a cheap gunny and start thinking before you dive in, Brogan?'

'Sorry, Mr King.'

'Never mind that. Go tell the sheriff I want to see him here in five minutes.'

'The sheriff, boss?'

'Are you deaf as well as dumb? Move, man, move!'

Brogan moved fast.

* * *

Navajo Joe packed an ancient nine-pound Hawkin rifle shaped like an old-fashioned buffalo-gun with an elongated stock and a tassled carry-loop.

Lucky Ned Pepper had amused himself over the last ten miles by insisting he would rather subject himself to multi impacted tooth removals without gas than be seen dead with such a travesty of a weapon in his possession.

The tracker had just smiled and nodded. Lucky Ned had scared the hell out of Greenhorn County's best tracker by this. He was a deeply relieved man upon sighting the ring of lights on the wide plain below when they emerged from Callaghan's Pass.

'Boiling Fork!' he announced triumphantly. 'Joe go now.'

'You still don't get it, do you, Sitting Bull? You don't go now — or ever — until I say so. And I ain't said so yet. How the hell do I know this town's like you say? And even if it is, how do I know that's where this bunch is heading, anyway? Seems to me — '

Lucky Ned broke off as Fletch caught his attention and gestured towards the distant lights.

'What?' The killer's tone was rough-edged and almost menacing. This trail had been too long and too hard for a man plagued by the greatest uncertainty concerning the biggest job he'd ever pulled. He'd barely slept since Cracker Creek, and because Fletch,

Poker Bill, Conneroy, Mex Tom and O'Toole had all ridden with him before, and knew what he could be capable of, none of them had got any rest worth a damn either. 'Well, don't just set your saddle there looking like a fool, man . . . '

'That map we seen at the trailhouse at Poker Flats, Ned. It showed Boiling Fork as the only town of any size inside fifty mile. When we lost the bunch's sign they were heading dead in this direction, so . . . '

He let his words fade. Pepper stared hard at him for a moment longer, then they saw his shoulders relax.

He spat in the dust and sleeved his mouth.

'OK, OK, then let's show some speed,' he grunted. 'Well, what are you waiting for?'

He led them off the knoll and weary horses kicked clouds of red dust against a gibbous moon. Lucky Ned Pepper calculated they should make the town by midnight.

'Do you like it?' Pop Harney asked gloomily, breaking a long silence.

Gar Brothers blew froth from his fresh beer and stared at the older man in puzzlement.

'Like what? You don't just set around swilling booze for half an hour without a word, then pipe up and say something like that. You sure you ain't getting senile, old man?'

'I'd sooner be senile than a Republican voter like you, any day.'

It had been that sort of long day and night. They'd had a noisy time of it in the town and the Nugget was still roaring at ten-thirty. Brothers was content to stay seated there atop the piano until daybreak if that was how the night played out, but Pop just could not relax.

There was a reason for that, and it glided past the pair now. Cassie King had shown up at the saloon two hours earlier and hadn't left Shannon's side more than once or twice since.

The two were giving other couples a lesson in how the Swiss polka should be done now, and when the young woman laughed at something Shannon said and tossed her auburn curls, Brothers felt like laughing right along with her.

Not his companion.

'Well, ain't you even gonna ask what's bothering me?' Pop asked.

'Him!' the older man continued, and jabbed his pipestem at a figure on the opposite side of the onlookers' circle. 'He was here, he went away for a spell, now he's back again. And you can see what he's staring at, can't you?'

Gar Brothers had to focus to see clearly. After a while he nodded. 'Uh-huh. You mean that Brogan joker who's watching them dance. So?'

'What's he use for brains?' came the rhetorical response. Then Pop Harney snorted. 'Don't you listen to any gossip, man? Her big rich daddy's got her all lined up to marry a geezer who could likely buy this whole town if he was of a mind, the rumour has it that King is going broke on account the seams are running out and his men are striking all the time . . . and you still can't see how Shan shining up to this daughter of his might be sending that big man loco right now?'

'Oh, is that all? I thought you might've been talking serious for a change. Hey, look, the dance has finished and they're heading for the bar. Hope they don't up and elope before the next polka, eh? Heh, hey!'

Drinkers made way for the dancers and Shannon signalled to the sweating barkeep for a rye and a sarsaparilla. He was perspiring lightly and was aware of a strange feeling that he couldn't identify at first. But as their drinks came through and they carried them to a table nearby, a bell rang in his head, and he realized he was simply happy.

That almost stopped him in his tracks.

Happiness was something he thought he'd said goodbye to the day the bunch was sworn in as cavalrymen of the Confederate States of America, seemingly an age ago now.

He'd barely been aware that it was one of many things in life that seemed to have simply been blown away along with all those lives, until tonight.

It was exciting yet, in a way, alarming.

That was his first reaction. His second was to tell himself not to be such a dramatist. They were simply dancing together and enjoying it — the rich man's daughter and the ex-guerilla fighter. Keep it simple, Shannon!

'Do they fun it up like this all the time here in Boiling Fork?' he asked lightly as they sat.

'Only when we're invaded, I think.' She smiled.

'Invaded?'

'Father worries we're being invaded by Yankees now the war is over,' she said lightly. She sipped her drink and added, 'I don't think it would surprise him if you and the others turned out to be Northerners posing as Southerners. He suspects everybody of just about everything.'

At that moment Barlow King was far down Shannon's list of conversational topics. He was still amazed at how it felt simply to spend an enjoyable evening free of tension and stress.

His eyes played around the crowded saloon, as he listened to what she was saying but he was observing everything sharply, gauging the atmosphere of his new home, familiarizing himself with its character and mood.

It would be foolish to rate Boiling Fork a typical south-western town, he knew. He'd witnessed the hunger and tensions arising from the ongoing hard times and unemployment, along with the violence associated with the apparently failing copper-mine.

There was poverty here and likely the future of the whole place was none too rosy.

But there he went again! Taking things too seriously. But the cure for that was at hand. He looked into Cassie King's eyes, the four-man band kicked in, and then they were back on the dance-floor again.

He didn't see anything significant in the fact that when they had circled once he looked for the man Cassie had referred to earlier as her 'watchdog', but big Jet Brogan was no longer seated at the bar.

The music changed tempo and when Cassie began to sing the words of 'Annie Laurie' he found himself humming along. Who would have believed it?

6

The Intruder

Cole Shannon lay on an ancient canvas cot in the storeroom of the High Tumbleweed ranch house, stretching his long legs beneath an old army blanket.

It was still dark, yet he knew it was close to morning. He stared up at the dim ceiling and listened to the rain on the roof. The heavy clouds had been coming in low and dark over the mesa last night when he was turning in. The rain wasn't heavy now, but steady. Good grass-growing rain he told himself, and grinned in the gloom.

He reckoned he was beginning to think and act more like a sodbusting rancher and less like an ex-soldier every day.

He clung to that thought a moment,

liking it. His life before the war had been hard and driven, the unforgettable four years of war chaotic and dominated by a single imperative. Survival.

In a strange way it almost felt sinful to lie abed in the dark of an early morning and not be afraid, or worse, ready to kill.

He discarded the thought and flung the blanket aside, swung his legs to the floor and reached for hat and boots.

A chorus of snores greeted him as he padded out along the hallway. Cocking his head he identified Pop Harney's tenor-toned snoring and Gar Brothers's bass.

Kit and Riley shared the main bedroom with Pop and Gar, but both youngsters slept quietly, Kit Quill because he was too young and Courtney likely on account he was too vain.

They were a mixed bunch, this six with whom he'd survived the war, and he idly wondered how unusual it might be that veterans should survive together this long after the war's end.

Maybe they were genuinely unique?

The first grey light was seeping through the window now as, boots still in hand, he paused to peer into the second room at the dim motionless shapes of Jack and Digger.

Though Cole had most always been first up and about in the army, Jack Quade had seldom been far behind. But right now he could tell the big man was in a deep sleep still, doubtless due to the long hours he was putting in along with everybody else. Some had been still up and playing cards when he'd retired. He didn't gamble himself. Not on cards, leastways. He'd have to rate this whole venture a gamble, but somehow he liked the odds.

He was thoughtful as he went through to the front room, closed the door behind him and sat down to draw on his boots.

Some were finding it pretty tough to adjust to the new way of life, he was well aware. He had little doubt that Jack, Pop and probably Digger would settle into the regular hours, hard work and lack of daily excitement without much difficulty. But he was far from certain about some of the others.

Gar, for example, had never been what could be deemed a worker. Highly skilled at fist-fighting or scrounging for rations behind enemy lines, but never a man for whom the mundane and repetitious held much appeal.

Kit Quill could work like an Irish navvy when in the mood, and the youngest of the bunch appeared to be taking to ranch life well enough, he supposed. But lack of excitement over time might prove a worry. Whoever coined the phrase 'he'd rather fight than eat' could well have had Kit in mind.

Then there was Riley.

Cole's expression grew sober now as he stood and drew on his leather jacket. How could anyone ever be sure how Court might react to any given situation? The man had been against their agreement concerning the gold from the start and had been often withdrawn and moody ever since. Shannon supposed that when it came right down to cases, that vain and even arrogant man with the lightning Colt and trigger temper might well be the hardest of the six to predict.

He washed in the kitchen then stepped out on to the front gallery to pause on the top step.

He inhaled deeply.

All around the world lay hushed, the land itself seeming to breathe softly in the gentle hour between night and day.

A moment like this was like a benign drug to a former fighting man. A man could genuinely believe there was no sin in the early mornings, no bad memories or ugliness in the world.

'Don't get carried away, Shannon,' he murmured with a grin. He came down to earth again by reminding himself there was work to be done, specifically today to repair the broken fence out along the pine ridge.

The past was growing more distant

every day now, he reflected as he tugged down his hat-brim and headed across the sleeping yard for the stables. He supposed as the years went by a man might expect to erase more and more of the savage years from memory until little was left; maybe just the name — Shannon's Brigade.

He drew up with a grin upon reaching the stables. He shook his head. How had he branched off along those lines again, when he had a goddamn fence to fix? 'That is all ancient history, Shannon,' he reminded himself aloud, and pushed through the door to saddle his horse.

The big animal was frisky in the early morning, and once clear of the headquarters Shannon let him run. They followed the south meadow to Blackwater Canyon then turned half-right at the lightning-split cottonwood and headed towards the boundary.

Reining the horse back to an easy lope he tugged out his cigars and was in the process of feeling his pockets for his vestas when he sighted the horse-tracks half-way up the grass slopes just below the timberline.

Although the sign was faint it was still plain enough to a trailsman's eye. Shannon hadn't been up along that slope below the timberline in several days, although others could have been.

The rain drew a metallic curtain across the strengthening light as he cut across the flat and started to ascend the slope.

The ground was soggy up here but Ulysses was a sure-footed animal. Soon Shannon found himself staring down at a single line of hoof-tracks which came in from the south, crossed the slope at an angle then vanished into the timber in the direction of the house.

The sign was fresh and the horse that left it wore shoes with diamond-head nails. None of their horses here was shod with nails of that type.

Mere minutes before, Shannon had been reflecting on how distant the war and all the uncertainties associated with it had seemed. Yet within a matter of seconds it was as if he were back in the hills of Tennessee, tense, alert and sniffing the air like a war horse at first scent of battle smoke.

Someone had ridden on to High Tumbleweed during the night!

Shannon hauled his sixgun before stepping down. A wind with a chill in it brushed against his face as he stood staring at the footprints for a time. Last night in the town he'd seemed aware of something more than simple suspicion and antagonism in the air. That feeling was accentuated here where he stood upon his own land looking at that set of bootprints leading off in the direction of the shelf of stone they called the Look-out.

A man invading your land could just as easily be a harmless bum as some low-life intent on doing you harm.

He strode across to the timberline, leading Ulysses. On reaching the trees he tethered the animal securely, then followed the intruder's sign into the timber.

He made no sound as he walked. It was like a flashback to the war days without armies or cannon thunder . . . just two men who might get to kill one another if that was how a situation unfolded.

He shook his head. No. That was then . . . this was now. Likely just some bum, he reassured himself and continued on. There was no sound now but the gently falling rain.

Where the timber began to thin he caught the occasional glimpse of the ranch's pasture lands far below. A natural clearing lay ahead which he approached with infinite caution. The open space was some fifty yards across and sloped upwards for something like the same distance to where a triangular slab of gray stone marked the beginning of the steeper slopes.

Nobody to be seen.

He hunkered down and waited.

The rain continued to come down

steadily and now a wind stirred the leaves, causing a cold drizzle to drip down. He angled his Colt muzzle down then drew the flap of his leather jacket over his hand to protect the weapon.

Another ten minutes drifted by.

A coil of smoke coming from the ranch-house chimney. Somebody was abroad now, most likely Jack or Pop. The thought of hot black coffee started his belly rumbling.

A pebble rattled close by.

He rose smoothly and eased towards the source of the sound, a heavy talus rock slab which lay canted between two bent trees some sixty feet distant.

His sixgun hammer clicked back on to full cock as he emerged from the cover. Darting forward swiftly now, he first caught a glimpse of a Stetson hat dripping with rain, then the tip of a rifle, eventually a wisp of tobacco smoke.

A tall man sat on a deadfall log with his back to him staring directly down upon the headquarters. His headquarters. It didn't look like any kind of bum from where he stood — he thought he might even be vaguely familiar. Shannon raised his cocked .45.

'Reach and turn around real slow!'

The man turned, but not slow. He spun fast in alarm, lean, big-nosed face twisting with shock and surprise.

Shannon likely looked just as surprised as he stared at the man wearing a sheriff's star.

★   ★   ★

It was Pop Harney, standing at the kitchen work bench spooning coffee into a pot, who first sighted Shannon riding in with the stranger. Pop let out a warning yell, and by the time Shannon was thrusting the pale-faced sheriff of Boiling Fork through the doorway ahead of him, the whole outfit had gathered in the front room.

Six men looked confounded as they stood looking Shannon's strange catch up and down — until the coffee-pot boiled over. Pop cursed and grabbed for the pot and Sheriff Hazelton reached up warily to remove his sodden hat. The lawman had not spoken since his capture, and appeared reluctant to do so now.

Shannon was hardly surprised.

'You want to say something now or when we parade you before the justice in town?' he demanded.

The lawman compressed thin lips and shook his head.

'Where'd you land him, Cole?' Courtney Riley wanted to know.

Cole explained. His report created even more puzzlement and not a little hostility.

'This just don't make any sense at all,' Kit Quill said tightly. He whipped his shooter from leather and made to ram it into the lawman's lean belly, but Shannon moved to brush him aside.

'No, he doesn't need that, Kit. On account you are ready to explain right now, aren't you, Sheriff? To us or the justice, take your pick.'

'All right . . . all damn right!' The captive moved to a chair and dropped into it. 'I was here checking on you to see if you mightn't be a bunch of outlaws.'

'Why would you figure that?'

The lawman looked up. 'The cut of your rig . . . young, proddy looking . . . all them guns. Then there was the way you get about town, real arrogant and cocky. I guess you just plain didn't shape up as any good to my way of thinking.'

'Why don't I believe you, mister?' Shannon cut in coldly. He leaned forward to rest the heels of his hands upon the chair, his face close to the peace officer's now. 'For your information, we all worked behind enemy lands in the war, Hazelton. Often our lives depended on being able to tell if someone was telling us the truth or not. You are not telling us the truth, and if you keep that up you might get to end up too sick and sorry to tell anybody anything, even if you wanted to. So what . . . ?'

The lawman appeared to collapse inwardly at that. He was a man under unusual pressure and suddenly it had grown too much. 'All right, all right. I . . . I was told to come keep a watch on you. Ordered, I guess is more the word.'

Shannon straightened and glanced at the others. Jack Quade jabbed a forefinger at the lawman.

'Ordered? Whose orders?'

The man compressed his lips, looked from face to face for a glimmer of softness or compassion, but found none.

'Look, it's really quite simple and straightforward. We figured you looked suspicious so the natural thing to do was for me to — '

'Just a minute,' interrupted Digger Morgan. 'You said 'we'. Tell me in plain honest Australian, who's we?'

The sheriff's last pause was by far his longest. Then he sighed and stared at the floor. 'Myself and Mr King.'

They traded startled looks. Then Shannon said, 'Barlow King . . . the mine owner?'

The lawman nodded and Gar Brothers stepped in closer.

'Why the hell should King be interested in us? And since when did a town sheriff start taking orders from citizens, badgepacker?'

Now Hazelton met their eyes. The man looked wretched. 'Mr King is a very powerful and forceful man, I'm afraid. As council chairman he's got the power to fire me if I don't measure up . . . or if I fail to do as I'm told. Guess it's always been that way in Boiling Fork, and it's gotten a whole lot worse since the seams began playing out and folks were suddenly getting laid off and half-starving and scared — '

'Why that dirty — ' Courtney Riley began, but Shannon cut him off.

'Never mind that, Court,' he said with quiet authority. Then he drew the sheriff's revolver from his own belt and handed it back to him. 'All right,

Sheriff, I now believe you've told us the truth. You are free to go.'

Hazelton blinked wonderingly as he got to his feet. 'You mean you'd let me go . . . just like that?'

'Not quite just like that.' Shannon folded his arms. 'We'll be riding back to town with you. All of us. We are going calling on King, all of us together. He's got a lot of explaining to do and questions to answer . . . a man you might say who likely needs some serious straightening out. And you are going to help us do that. Right?'

'He's got nary an objection,' Courtney Riley drawled. He spun his sixgun on his trigger finger, flipped it into the air and caught it on his little finger without even looking then slipped the piece expertly into its holster. 'Keerect, Sheriff?'

Sweating now, Hazelton ran a finger around his shirt collar. 'Correct . . . I guess,' conceded the most miserable looking man in Paiute County.

7

Strangers with Guns

They were not expecting her today, so she was prepared to wait some time before she might get to see any sign of life.

The rain had blown away and there was sunlight on the hills beyond the ghoster, soft sunlight that dappled the trees and cast gentle shadows across the thinning grass.

It was quiet in Warcloud. It usually was but for the occasional stage that rumbled along the long and narrow main stem running to or from Boiling Fork, seven miles to the south-east.

Mostly she enjoyed the quiet as a refreshing relief from both the hurly-burly of the mining town and the tension and tantrums of her home.

Her father constantly reminded her

how fortunate she was to live in the very finest home in all Paiute County. He never seemed to comprehend it took more than grand pianos, inch-thick floor carpets and servants to transform a house into a home.

To her way of thinking the King mansion on Duel Street had never quite made that transition, and she doubted it ever would. Not now.

'Now' was a particularly bad time at the big house for everyone in it, and the daughter of the house believed it was worse for her than anybody else.

That thought pulled her up as she walked slowly by the old hotel in her jodhpurs and riding-boots. She shouldn't complain, she chided herself — not even when her father was being impossible which he was almost constantly these days.

Small wonder, she supposed. Couldn't be much fun watching your profit margins tumble. Or to be fighting with your workers, quarrelling with the bank and trying your damnedest to convert a courtship into a marriage.

Cassie King shook her head at that last thought. Her ongoing 'spinsterhood', as her parent chose to label it, was becoming an increasingly tetchy point between father and daughter. He simply could not understand her reasons for continually keeping the finest catch in the county at arm's length.

She sighed.

Of course she was quite fond of Quentin Kaley, who was undeniably handsome, a gentleman and, of course, rich.

She grimaced as she recommenced her stroll.

She was in no way averse to money either. But why couldn't her father understand that a girl could not be herded into a marriage like a beast being run into the marshalling yards in town?

And why Barlow's sudden obsession with Cole Shannon? She'd had tall and handsome admirers before, but her parent had mostly just sniffed at these, then advised her to 'lift her sights' and find somebody better.

Until she had 'found' her rich and handsome suitor from down-valley, that was.

Ever since then Barlow seemed to have little else on his mind, outside the horrendous decline of the mine, than presiding over her nuptials.

Trouble was, she understood why all too clearly. Money. Her admirer's family were loaded, while Barlow appeared to be in an increasingly worsening financial bind.

She supposed she understood the pressure he was under right now. But was that any reason to treat her like a prize heifer to be traded off to the first buyer with enough wealth to save the family fortunes?

She halted at a sound. As a regular visitor here she was keenly attuned to this slightly spooky 'ghost town.' This was essential, for the people who lived their secret lives up here on the south trail dare not show themselves for fear that it would be reported and someone, quite possibly her father, would insist the sheriff move them on.

Her image danced in a dusty store window. How rich and fashionable she must look to the poor, she mused. And wondered just how long she would be able to maintain this façade if her father's fortunes did not improve, or if she failed to marry moneybags Quentin Kaley.

And as so often these days when Kaley came to mind, she found herself comparing him with Cole Shannon, mystery man from High Tumbleweed Ranch.

And today, as had happened every such moment lately, that tall somewhat mysterious newcomer dominated her interest in a way her more conventional admirer never had.

She walked on quickly for half a block, which took her past the Days of Glory saloon, Arbuckle's Furnishings, the falling-down City Billiard Parlour and the burnt-out remains of the once flourishing Quality Restaurant and Wine Rooms, to reach eventually the alleyway where a whispered greeting sounded on the still air.

'Missy Cassie!'

She halted to glance both ways before darting into the alleymouth with her basket on her arm, smiling happily when she saw the children emerge from the shadows.

There were six or seven of them ranging from teenagers down to a curly-headed toddler. They were the children of the adults who lived and hid further back from the main road, some twenty or thirty all told, mostly Mexican or coloured, all victims of the war-whipped racism that had led Boiling Fork to drive all such newcomers from that town in order to keep white men employed at the mine.

Some would have perished but for King's daughter. Somehow she always managed to keep them supplied, while at the same time fighting for a change in council policy back in town.

Naturally her father knew nothing of any of this, although he frequently expressed puzzlement at how quickly domestic supplies appeared to dwindle in his house.

Cassie had managed to smuggle out a few extras today, and by the time she quit the alley thirty minutes later the children had been fed, pampered, reassured and promised things would improve dramatically for them 'sometime soon'.

Guilt accompanied Cassie King as she returned to the main street to head for the yard where she always left her horse. She meant every word she had said, yet none knew better than she just how difficult and probably impossible any kind of improvement might be for the 'ghosts' of this ghost town.

With the town falling behind her she followed the main trail down the slopes of the hills and soon found herself approaching the junction with the old North-west Trail.

She was thinking of nothing much in

particular and enjoying the ride, when through the thinning timber ahead she glimpsed riders approaching the junction from the north, making for her destination, Boiling Fork.

Alarm bells rang.

At a distance the horsemen appeared well mounted and rode with a certain arrogance, not unusual in this masculine environment. But two things caught her attention immediately and caused her to slow, then stop.

The first was the unusual number of weapons, both rifles and revolvers, the second, the man riding ahead.

She focused on the leader as he approached the intersection some fifty yards ahead of his party. He rode very upright in the saddle and his features were pale, strong and handsome in a chilling kind of way.

The party failed to see her where she held her mount steady in the tree shade off the shoulder of the trail, and she gave them several minutes to disappear before emerging.

Everything was simply getting worse by the day, she thought in a rare moment of self-pity. Riots at the mines and occasional gunfights within the town itself; her father increasingly difficult and bitter; tension, brawling, drunkenness all on the rise. And now a whole squad of fresh trouble coming in from the tall and uncut.

Where would it all end?

And then another very different kind of query took her completely by surprise. When might she see Cole Shannon again?

* * *

'Maybe we'd better be heading back, Court?'

'I'm not through here yet.'

'You know, with Shan and the others all going over to face King and all, mebbe it was a bit . . . you know . . . weak for us to quit on them?'

Anger flushed Courtney Riley's handsome features.

155

'Riley never quits nothing, mister. I pulled out because I knew it was going to be all jawbone again, no action. It's plain as paint to me that King is big enough in this town to use the sheriff like a hired hand to set him spying on the bunch. And all Shan plans to do is talk to the sonova and try and scare him by rattling the judge at him. No action, nothing but jawbone. Not good enough for this child, which is why there's no way I was going to waste my time tagging along. Hey, barkeep, two more!'

Silence fell over the back bar.

Young Kit Quill stood watching as his companion fished money from his pocket and started counting to pay the barman.

Riley glanced up at him from beneath winged black brows.

'Yeah, you're right, I'm short of cash and I've got that good-looker from the hotel panting for me to show her a time, and what can I do with nickels and dimes? You know I've good mind to — '

He broke off suddenly upon noticing two husky men in the corner staring their way. Miners in big broken boots and sporting stubbled jaws.

'What?' Riley rapped, straightening to face the pair. 'You Cousin Jacks got something on your mind, maybe?'

The men bristled. They were big rough dudes down on their uppers who found these young newcomers way too flash and cocky for their taste.

'Maybe,' replied the larger, setting his pint glass aside. 'Maybe I was just looking at you rare birds and asking my pard here if someone had kicked the slop bucket over . . . mebbe.'

Riley cursed and charged.

The big miner was surprisingly quick on his feet. He evaded the first wild charge and countered with a rabbit-punch to the back of the neck that put Courtney Riley down on one knee. A big boot lashed at his head but Riley ducked under, then exploded upright, using his head as a battering ram to catch his adversary under the jaw. The man's head snapped back and Riley slammed two lightning blows to the mid section. When the dazed brawler buckled forward in agony, Riley linked both hands together, lifted them high then brought them crunching down on the back of the neck in a brutal rabbit-killer blow.

The miner slammed into the floor with his face and didn't even kick.

Meantime Quill reached the second man and sent him reeling with an elbow jolt to the chin. The Cousin Jack had a cast-iron jaw. He retaliated with one round-house right that missed its mark and a battering-ram straight left that did not. Quill hit the floor and was struggling to rise when Riley kicked his attacker's feet from beneath him, dropping him to his knees. Rising swiftly, Quill swung a kick that caught his man in the side of the face and snapped his jaw. As he cried out in agony, Riley casually swept up a chair and broke it over his head with a shattering crash that felled him unconscious.

By this the door was jammed with goggle-eyed onlookers who watched the High Tumbleweed pair collect their hats. In an instant the doorway cleared and they sauntered outside unchallenged into the afternoon light, swaggering a little for the benefit of the onlookers.

'Best fun I've had since the Army paid us off, pard,' Riley remarked, dabbing at a cut lip.

They halted and Quill looked back. 'More miners coming our way . . .'

'I've had my fill of miners for one day. Let's go see how Shan's getting on with Mr High-Pockets King.'

'Yeah, OK . . . but I ain't any too sure he's going to be happy about this ruckus.'

'I've got something to tell you, man,' the other responded as they started off for the Duel Street corner. 'What makes Cole happy or unhappy doesn't exactly stoke my boilers much any longer.'

Kit Quill looked startled. 'What do you mean by that, pard?'

Riley turned his handsome head to

face him squarely. 'It means I'm not cut out for this cowboy life on the freaking range, boy. That I didn't risk my life every day with the Brigade just so I could get to punch cows and fork horseshit on a spread with a fortune in yellow gold underneath it. You want to hear any more?'

Kit Quill decided he'd heard enough, for now. He hooked thumbs in his shell-belt and glanced over his shoulder. The angry miners had dropped back, settling for shouting curses after them rather than giving chase. He grinned, squared his shoulders and swung ahead to see thin sunlight glinting from the metal rain-catchers on the roof of the King mansion.

★ ★ ★

'A case could be brought against you for forcing a council-appointed peace officer to break the law,' Shannon accused, pacing to and fro across the lush carpet of the study. 'And don't try and tell us you're not aware of that. I won't buy it.'

Seated behind his oaken desk, Barlow King made a tent with his fingers and studied Cole Shannon over it. The big man appeared calmer now, certainly much calmer than when the High Tumbleweed party had arrived with Judge Parker in tow and virtually forced their way into his house. That had been hard to take and he might have been tempted to summon all his men and have the 'offenders' ejected but for the presence of the judge.

For should the event on High Tumbleweed reach the courts, this town's premier citizen believed he would find himself standing on very shaky ground. He had enough concerns without that. More than enough.

'I was quite within my rights,' he declared firmly. 'I have been beset with difficulties here in recent times, and you and your gang's unheralded arrival and subsequent unsettling activities only served to exacerbate the situation. I sought the sheriff's assistance to — '

'He wasn't hiding up there on private property spying on honest citizens to assist anything lawful,' accused Pop Harney, a wily man with an educated background. 'So why don't you just admit you've both broken the law and undermined its authority, Mr King, and maybe we can go on from there.'

King looked appealingly at the judge, but Parker just cleared his throat and glanced away. The man was covertly studying his 'escort'. Judge Parker could be a formidable man to deal with in the courthouse, but was finding being up close and personal with several of the most formidable 'veterans' he'd ever been involved with, quite a different story.

A side door swung open and Jet Brogan strode in followed by a trio of mansion employees.

'All right, that'll be enough of this,' the hard man snapped. 'You've had your gripe, now you're all through.' He jerked a thumb over his shoulder. 'Get!'

Shannon turned and put a hard stare on the man. But Brogan did not scare easily. He motioned to a hatchet-faced sidekick who lifted his rifle threateningly.

Shannon did not scare either.

'Better tell him I can draw and kill him before he could squeeze trigger, hired help!' His voice was cold, his right hand resting on gun handle. Seconds stalked the tense stillness before King motioned urgently to the hand, who angled his rifle down with a sigh of relief.

But Shannon waited until the hand actually set the weapon aside before returning to business at hand.

'Let's stop shilly-shallying, King. We both know what was behind this fool play of yours. Don't we?'

'I don't know what you're talking about.'

Shannon drew closer to the desk.

'We're talking about your daughter and — '

'How dare you, sir!'

'I dare right enough. It's the only explanation that makes sense. Cassie and I've struck up a friendship and you've got her lined up to marry someone else. So you used your 'lawman in the pocket' pal here to spy on me in the hope of coming up with something you could use against me and likely get rid of me, if I'm any guess. So, go ahead and tell me I'm wrong.'

'Damn your impertinence, you . . . you — '

'It's so and you know it,' Shannon cut him off, swinging to the gaunt man in sober black. 'I had you along so you'd have a first-hand understanding of what happened out on the spread, Judge. You'll note King hasn't denied the charges . . . likely believes he's so big he doesn't have to. But if you're not deeply concerned about a citizen treating a peace officer like a hired hand, then you sure should be.'

Parker cleared his throat. 'I shall draft a report on this whole extraordinary affair and submit it to head office in Claytontown before — '

'I'm sure you will.'

Shannon was sarcastic. He was beginning to wonder whether a man strong and ruthless enough to have a town sheriff running odd jobs for him might not be above having a judge on his payroll. This was some town! But even as that thought presented itself, he knew there was no way he would quit. He was here to stay. If Paiute County was not up to his standards, he would stay on and fight until it changed.

He turned for the doors. Brogan blocked his way. King's bodyguard was the one citizen he'd seen here who shaped up to Shannon's assessment of a genuine hard man.

Their eyes met and locked for a second time and for a moment the tension was explosive. Then King made a sound in his throat, Brogan gave Shannon a final icy glare, then stepped aside.

Shannon led the way to the big

double doors, then paused and turned. 'You've acted like a fool, King. If there is a next time . . . ' He let that hang in the air. 'OK, let's go, boys.'

They left.

It seemed quite a walk to the front doors and they didn't relax until they were standing on the gallery in the late afternoon light. They sensed eyes watching from windows and doorways but there was no attempt to hinder their leaving.

As they strode on down the paved pathway for the gate a rider appeared at the fence. It was Cassie King on her long-legged bay.

'Cole!' she said, surprised. 'What . . . ?'

'Your dad and I just had a little business to talk over,' he said with a grin. He glanced back to see an angry face disappear from a window, turned back to her. He was serious now. 'Sorry about this. Your father will likely tell you about it. I don't want you to think the worse of us because of it.'

'I couldn't do that.' She turned to

glance along the street. 'Have you sighted any unusual-looking strangers in town, Cole?'

'No. Why?'

She shrugged.

'When I was coming back from my ride I saw a party travelling this way and they . . . well, they looked so wild and dangerous I thought, particularly the man leading them.' She turned back, forcing a smile. 'Perhaps we're all getting a little nervous and jumpy these days. Shall I be seeing you soon?'

'Bet on it, Cassie.' He smiled and led his men off down the street.

With so much on his mind, he didn't dwell upon the party the girl had seen. But in time he would.

For Lucky Ned Pepper had come to town.

8

Trouble Town

The unemployed miners were hungry and threadbare yet still managed a certain swagger and defiance as they came marching in ranks down Main. Some toted lanterns and there was a hint of the military about their ragged ranks. Their singing was far less impressive:

'Oh we're boys from the old
    Monte Cristo!
We worked for nickels and dimes,
Then Barlow King sacked us,
We're now eating cactus,
But we're having the greatest of
    times.
Oh yeah!'

The song broke off in a ragged yell and the crowds lining the plankwalks cheered or jeered, depending on where they stood in the ever worsening situation at the faltering copper-mine.

The tall and solemn stranger in the long dark duster and turned-down hat stood motionless, watching the ragged cavalcade go by, face devoid of expression. There was a crash of glass as some fool heaved a rock through a store window, this action drawing lustier cheering, then the beginning of another verse.

Haig Marlowe inhaled and flexed travel-weary limbs. His rifle was heavy tonight but was never a burden. He hefted it easily and limped off along the walk in search of suitable accommodation.

The United States Treasury Department's top field operative was typical of his unique species. The special unit boasted not a single flashy operator or gung-ho treasure-chaser amongst its ranks. But men like Marlowe were unsung heroes back in Washington DC and it had selected one of its best to hunt down its missing $10,000 in gold coin.

The gold had gone missing following a murderous attack on an Army pay train in the dying days of the war. The appointee had proved unable to pick up its trail for some time until his tracking skills eventually led him to a grisly death scene at a place named Cracker Creek.

In his solitary and remorseless way the veteran of a hundred such hunts had eventually caught the scent of a bunch of riders he took to be outlaws, who in turn were conducting a relentless pursuit of another slightly larger group which kept leading them on into the south-western regions, eventually to reach Paiute County and the remote mining town of Boiling Fork.

Agent Marlowe was exhausted that night, but didn't let it show. In his dangerous line of work he was often mistaken for an unimaginative plodder, for that was the persona he displayed as he went quietly from one highly successful assignment to another.

But behind the grey exterior was a man of steely temperament and ruthless ability who'd cut his eye-teeth in the Service hunting down thieves and brigands who almost invariably turned murderously defiant and dangerous when cornered.

Treasury expected its field operatives both to get its man and to stay alive. Thus far in his career, Haig Marlowe had shown himself highly successful at both.

The current case had been one of the agent's longest and most testing assignments. Yet he sensed trail's end might be near now as he made his inconspicuous way along the warped plankwalks of Boiling Fork.

He was all but staggering from exhaustion yet still noted every man he met during that walk. Having maintained contact from long distance with his quarry as hunter and hunted crossed a wide sweep of southern Texas, he could not identify any of them here even if they were to come face to face.

Then why waste time studying every man he encountered?

Simple. He was mainly glancing at their feet. For he'd been studying the footprints the manhunters left in their wake all the long way from Cracker Creek along with the even fainter, older tracks of the seven riders whom the others in turn were trailing south.

He failed to sight any footwear or peculiar walking gaits that might link somebody to either bunch. He was in no way discouraged or disappointed. The one thing Treasury never did was set its field men time limits. Any given hunt might take a day or six months. Marlowe had been fully engaged on this operation for five long weeks, yet plodding along tonight in Boiling Fork he was encouraged by the belief his hunt would end here.

★　★　★

172

Lucky Ned bounced down the hotel stairs next morning with a spring in his step and a fragrant corona clamped between smiling teeth.

He'd slept like a saint and looked it.

Guests and staff in the shabby lobby looked at him curiously as he sauntered through, for he was flashy and cocky in a style that was unusual in this rough and ready mining town.

'Who's that?' someone queried, and a clerk behind the desk responded, 'Name's Smith — he says.'

Even though the place was a dump, it was the top hotel in town. Pepper was the only member of the bunch putting up here, having consigned his henchmen to a clapboard wreck on the southern fringe of town frequented by stumblebums and miners.

By the time midnight had rolled around the killer knew almost as much about Boiling Fork as did its average citizen. He'd made it his business to do so, for he would be playing for high stakes here and didn't intend to make any slip-ups simply because he hadn't done his groundwork.

For instance, when he paused out front to soak up a few warming rays, he could tell at a glance what passing miners still had a job at the Monte Cristo and which did not. He glimpsed a man sporting the five-pointed star across the street and instantly knew he had next to nothing to fear from that quarter.

His judgement was that good, and needed to be.

Two horsemen clattered by. The one with broad shoulders and rat-trap jaw gave him a challenging stare. Pepper ran through his memory file and muttered, 'Brogle . . . no, Brogan. King's standover merchant and the guy the Cousin Jacks fear most . . .'

His lip curled in a sneer. Small-town heroes! Tenth-raters like Brogan wouldn't know what hit them once Lucky Ned got started!

And talking about getting started . . .

He tilted his hat against a probing

sun and rubbed his hands together to get rid of the chill as he strode off south along Main, a ramrod-erect figure with a swagger who drew the eye, impressing towners as somebody who managed to appear both interesting and slightly intimidating at the same time.

He didn't waste a moment upon reaching El Dumpo, as he called it. The boys were still sluggish and aching from all those miles, but they quickly sharpened up when he sat them down and started in talking.

Every instinct told Lucky Ned this town was trail's end and he wasn't about to waste any time getting his hands on his gold.

'All right, let's see who was paying attention last night, you layabouts. What's High Tumbleweed?'

A couple stared blankly. They were groggy and sick and the leader's edgy energy was intimidating.

Then Navajo Joe spoke up. 'Where seven are.'

'At least someone's awake.' Pepper

began pacing to and fro before them across the bare boards of the lobby. There was nobody else about. Folks slept late here; it helped chew up part of a day with nothing to do.

The number seven had been important to the killer dating all the way back to Cracker Creek where he'd found the buried bodies of the original caretakers of his thieved gold shot to doll-rags. Right from the get-go, the Indian had claimed they were hunting a party of seven, and when some sharp questioning of the locals here by Pepper the night before had delivered the information that a bunch of exactly that number had quite recently taken up a lease on an outlying ranch, his eyes had lit up like a horse player watching his choice bolt home by the length of the straight.

This might prove even easier than he'd figured.

'OK,' he said soberly. 'This is what we gotta do. First up, Joe, you're riding out to the north to look over that ranch set-up — and you'll see everything and remember everything and nobody will catch one whiff of you — hear? You can take one or two with you but just make double certain you ain't sighted. The rest of you can spread around town, keep your eyes and ears open, pick up anything you can, and stay out of trouble. Got it?'

Heads nodded. Then Navajo Joe said: 'What you do, boss?'

'Why, look for the opening, of course.'

'What's that?' Conneroy queried, licking a cylinder of rice-paper and tobacco together.

'When you got more than one geezer involved in anything anywhere,' Pepper lectured, 'then you've got the chance of an opening, a chink in the wall. With seven men, there's got to be weak links . . . plenty opportunities for a smart operator like me to sniff out a weakness. Would you believe I've already scented one or two in this Shannon geezer's bunch?'

They were impressed; they had to be. 'Such as, boss?' croaked Poker Bill, fully awake at last.

'Two young fellers from High Tumbleweed have been drinking up big in town here and moaning and groaning about how they hate ranching and suchlike, while it seems the rest of the bunch has settled in fine. To me that's a chink that calls for prising open, and mebbe I'll get to do it.'

He was gone before they realized he'd finished. They stared at one another and grinned. When any man rode with Lucky Ned Pepper he always had that feeling he'd backed a winner.

★ ★ ★

Cole Shannon continued to spoon Pop's good soup from the bowl and Courtney Riley kept talking. Nobody else in the ranch-house kitchen moved or spoke. The outfit had known some dramatic moments over the years but nothing like this. No man had ever quit before.

'We've given it a good try-out here,' Riley continued. 'Kit and me, that is. But, hell, you never heard me craving to be a cowboy sitting a bad horse in the rain all day, did you? I don't know what I figured we'd do when it was all over, but it sure wasn't this. So, we've talked it over and that's it. We're quitting.'

Shannon looked up and said, 'Good soup.'

Riley flushed.

'Now don't start being smart, Shan, on account I've never been more serious in my life — '

'No, it really is fine soup,' Shannon said, rising. He looked the younger man squarely in the eye. 'OK.'

Riley blinked.

'That's it?'

Shannon moved to the fireplace and took out the makings.

'I never had to press any man to stay in the bunch during the fighting, and I'm not starting now, Court. You've been a top Brigader, none better, and I'm going to miss you. Kit, too. But I guess I saw this coming and more or less got ready for it. We're all pretty bushed tonight, so what say we bring the gold up and count out your shares tomorrow?'

He paused to grin.

'Then maybe we'll all have a drink or two? How does that sound?'

Riley and Quill traded glances. They had expected fireworks and this was hugely anticlimactic. Then when Pop, Gar and the others lined up to shake hands and wish them well, the deadliest and the youngest soon-to-be-ex fighters of Shannon's Brigade realized to their surprise that this was one of the hardest things they'd ever had to do.

★ ★ ★

The sheriff halted the stranger on the street.

'Er, mind giving me your name and

your business here in Boiling Fork, mister?'

The lawman was right on the job today. His stock had never been lower. Word of his involvement with Barlow King had spread and citizens were calling for his dismissal. He felt that if he made himself visible and was seen to be busy he might have a chance of surviving a difficult time.

'Edward Clancy, Sheriff,' came the brisk reply. 'I'm in the gun business.'

'Guns?'

'Selling and buying, of course. Just between you and me I hate the things, but a man has to make a living. Right, Sheriff?'

'Er, yes, I suppose. And those fellows I saw you with at the saloon, Mr Clancy . . . ?'

'Guns too. All work for the same company, and we hope to make some good sales here. Real nice talking with you, Sheriff.'

'Yeah, you too, Mr Clancy.'

'Did I lie?' grinned Lucky Ned

Pepper when he related the story to his henchman at the Deuce a short time later. 'Told him I was Edward Clancy, which is the truth. Just left off the Pepper, is all.'

They chuckled and then the conversation turned serious. Each had been busy since their arrival and by this were all of the one mind concerning their quarry.

'It can only be that bunch on the High Tumbleweed Ranch we took a good long look at, Ned,' insisted tall Fletch, leaning an elbow on the bar. 'Newcomers from the north and all likely-looking . . . I seen one on the street earlier. And of course, there's seven of them. Reckon that's still the clincher, right?'

Heads nodded in agreement. There were four present now — Fletch, Poker Bill, Conneroy and Navajo Joe.

The Indian rolled his rogue eyes and nodded emphatically. 'You bet,' he agreed. 'When this man pointed out one of the seven newcomers I checked out his prints in the sand and they match up with the prints we saw on our way from Cracker Creek.'

Lucky Ned lit up, inhaled deeply, exhaled luxuriously. It had been a long, hard manhunt but he'd stuck to it and could feel victory within his grasp.

Yet it had been a salutary journey and the outlaw knew he was a smarter and wiser man than the Lucky Ned who'd set off after the gold-snatchers from Cracker Creek weeks earlier. You learned a lot about a party when you tracked them over vast distances, and he now believed his quarry were hard, smart and resourceful and certainly in no way to be taken lightly.

Having caught a glimpse of the new crew on High Tumbleweed in town, the outlaw was still full of confidence, yet the caution factor had raised its unwelcome head.

Shannon's bunch looked the real deal. Just a glimpse was enough for him to understand how come his initial gold-couriers had wound up in those shallow graves at that grassy bend in Cracker Creek.

In a strangely pensive mood he studied his henchmen, couldn't help speculating whether they were up to the task now he'd seen the enemy.

In order to shake off the uncertainty that could plague even him when plotting a major job, he first visited his quarters then took his tensions for a walk.

He sensed that Boiling Fork seemed even a little more tense and unsettled than it had been upon their arrival, as he made his way out to the hump in the trail from which could be seen the distant smokes and dust of the copper-mine.

He'd heard more talk today about the rumoured mine closure following more sackings and another attempted mine-burning. Barlow King was said to be reinforcing his retinue of enforcers and bodyguards.

He was interested in King; he always was where the rich were concerned.

The citizens seemed of one mind that King had been needlessly harsh in the way he'd mistreated his workforce and laid half of them off. But after sizing up the riff-raff Mr Big had sacked, he couldn't say he blamed the man.

It wasn't until some time later, as he charmed a couple of floozies who found him interestingly different, that he was apprised of some of the more personal problems that King was facing in these troublesome times.

They said the big man was really doing it tough on a financial level. So tough in fact that he was strenuously attempting to advance his daughter's mooted wedding to a likely suitor from a genuine big-dollar family from a neighboring town.

The latest rumour was that Cassie King had only recently met and had taken immediate interest in one Cole Shannon, new lessee of High Tumbleweed Ranch.

'They say Mr King is angry enough about this to eat his shorts,' said the younger one, giggling. 'And I guess that's easy enough to understand, when you look at how stinking rich that Kaley family is supposed to be. And I guess this Shannon feller, tall, dark and handsome though he surely is, can't be too flush or he wouldn't be wandering around leasing places like the High Tumbleweed. That seem to make sense to you, Mister . . . what was that cute name of yours again . . . ?'

'Edward Clancy,' the outlaw said vaguely, already moving off. For suddenly his mind was working in overdrive. The High Tumbleweed seven were his party — he was virtually sure of it now. But suddenly they looked more of a handful than he'd figured. Maybe he needed more men to pull this job off? Men and muscle who could be dumped the moment he had what he'd come for.

The name 'Barlow King' popped into his thinkbox almost immediately.

He considered a possibility, amazed by his own inventiveness and daring.

But how could he interest King and

his men in his coming showdown with Shannon's seven without letting Mr Big catch a whiff of the gold?

He decided to concentrate on that later. The more he considered his idea the better it seemed to take shape. King could help him, and he could promise to help the big man in return. With luck and careful planning he might be back in possession of his stolen US Treasury gold and be half-way to Mexico before King would realize he'd gone.

He smiled secretively as he made his way across the street to a smaller bar where he ordered a jolt of their finest. He reckoned he'd just earned it.

★ ★ ★

The autumn was coming on, winter would not be far behind. Two days had passed since the showdown scene with Riley and Quill, yet the pair had made no move to collect their share of the gold and head on . . . to wherever and whatever that might prove to be. Pop

Harney was down with the colic and Gar Brothers was doing a lousy job as stand-in cook. Yet Shannon seemed content to go about his regular ranch chores just as though nothing special was going on at the High Tumbleweed.

This wasn't far from the truth, at least as far as Shannon was concerned. He'd learned during the war to take things as they came, and what came to him that day was the job of hazing the small gather of yearlings he'd bought from the neighbouring spread around Ghost Canyon and along the single-track trail for Yellow Butte Pasture.

Already he was growing familiar with both names and terrain. None of the others seemed half as keen as himself on such matters. This bothered him not at all. Some still liked to give the impression they were making up their minds about the future, yet he would bet money that in the final wind-up, all but the younger ones would stay on.

The day was growing colder and the young beeves were frisky. Tugging his hat low against the cut of the wind, Shannon found himself nodding to himself. He might well be in the centre of a tumultuous time of change for the bunch, and there was a great deal that remained undecided and uncertain.

Yet he was as relaxed as a regular cattleman with nothing more to concern himself with than the beef prices.

Did that indicate he possessed a more equable temperament than he'd ever suspected? Or could it be that he had recently become that rare creature, a man who'd at last found where he belonged and wanted to be? And in that rare mood, he knew he didn't want to think about the gold, yet it was hard not to.

He knew he'd never wanted it, suspected that at least some of the others felt the same.

He'd known right from Cracker Creek that he'd have been perfectly happy to have simply ridden off after that sixgun showdown and just leave the stuff where it lay.

He wasn't superior to the notion of being rich, but only if he earned it or it came with no strings attached.

Their 10,000 dollars' worth failed on both those test points. But of course he'd had no option but to go with the majority at the time. Now he wished he hadn't, for the Brigade was on the verge of break-up due solely to that stash sunk down the old well.

He worried that the whole outfit might crumble and break up after Court and Kit had quit. The seven had been the nucleus of the constantly changing Shannon's Brigade for over a year before the surrender. That had become its basic structure. Seven, not five, two or whatever.

He was surprised to find a rugged-up Digger Morgan waiting for him when he reached Yellow Butte. The Australian greeted him with his trademark grin and after settling the young stuff and wiring up the gate, they headed back by way of Bald Knob.

'Been trying to figure something,

Cole . . . ' Digger said thoughtfully as they began to climb.

'What?' He hoped the man wasn't going to discuss the rift. That had been talked out and then some.

'Whether it's autumn in Australia too?'

'Well, don't look at me. What would I know about Australia, man? What would anybody?'

'You wouldn't be hard-mouthing the greatest country on earth by any chance, pard?'

Shannon clamped up. He'd been lured down that track before. Morgan liked to get you started on something like his home country, which nobody knew anything about, then take over the conversation and start in bragging about the place until you wanted to shoot him to shut him up.

He found himself smiling as they rode on. It was maybe the first time he'd done so since the boys told him they planned to go.

★ ★ ★

That night when Courtney Riley returned to the High Tumbleweed at 3.20 a.m. he found Shannon sitting on the stoop chewing an unlit cigarette.

As full of energy at that hour as he would be at breakfast, Riley bounced out of his saddle and flashed his trademark grin.

'Shucks, Mom, you didn't have to wait up for me and all.'

There was no answering smile from Shannon. He'd a busy night, after coming to a decision.

'Still thinking of pulling out I guess, Court?'

Riley sobered and leaned a hand against a stanchion. 'More than likely . . . I guess.'

'Figured.' Shannon was silent a moment then got to his feet. 'Well, I know it's going to be hard for you when you decide to go, so we've made it a bit easier for you.' He nodded towards the well beyond the ranch yard, dimly visible by starlight. 'Pop and I hauled the stash up and made up two sacks containing yours and Kit's shares. They're there for the taking any time you might decide to go. We're still hoping you don't, but . . . '

His voice trailed away. He'd lost more good men than he cared count in the war years, but none had ever quit the Brigade before. But then, there'd never been peace or a cache of yellow gold before, either.

'Mighty white of you, Shan.' Riley cleared his throat; it was an awkward moment. 'You got a bottle going in there by any chance?'

'Let's go take a look,' Shannon said, and threw an arm about the younger man's shoulders as they crossed the gallery.

9

The Last Day

Wilson kicked his horse to catch up with Brogan as they rode up into Boiling Fork from the river. As they passed by the smouldering ruin of the Chinese laundry opposite the blacksmith's, Brogan swore under his breath then cut his gaze up ahead. A knot of men stood beneath the awning of Clayton's Hardware. Miners. Or to be more accurate, as Wilson soon realized, ex-miners.

Monroe's bunch had been laid off at the mine the previous Friday, and the leader had a bad reputation which hadn't improved any as the situation at the Monte Cristo mine deteriorated.

Wilson shot a nervous glance at his companion as the gap closed. It was impossible to read Brogan's expression, other than that he looked at least as hard and uncompromising as he did most times, whether things were going badly or well.

The miners fell silent as the riders approached. One had his arm in a sling and another sported a black eye. They looked like, and were, part of the growing unemployed faction which had been involved in most of the troubles the town had seen in recent times.

'Er, don't forget we gotta meet the stage bringing Miss Cassie's feller to town, Jet.'

'I don't forget nothing, boy. Like I don't forget it was some of these sons of bitches who started that riot last Saturday.'

The day was chill but sweat gleamed on Wilson's face. When he'd first signed on with King things had been relatively normal in Boiling Fork. Seemed a long time ago, yet he realized it had only been several weeks.

The horsemen drew abreast of the group, who gave them stare for stare. As they passed on by a man let fly with a curse and bent down to pick up a stone.

Faster than fast, Brogan brought his horse wheeling around. He kicked it forward just as the miner was straightening. The big animal slammed into the man and sent him flying backwards to crash into an upright with sickening force. He slumped to the ground.

In a moment the miner's companions were cursing and rushing at the rider. But Brogan was ready — he could have been born ready, judging by the way he whipped out a sixgun and began chopping left and right, splitting faces and cracking heads in a whirlwind of blinding action which a gaping Wilson could hardly follow.

Suddenly those still on their feet cut and ran, one yelling back over his shoulder: 'We'll get you for this, Brogan you bastard! You and King! We'll . . . '

His voice was swallowed by another shot and he went ashen as he felt the slug whip close.

'Look me up anytime, scum!' Brogan

called after them. Then, seemingly calm again, he holstered the .45 and the two rode on.

Another day, another brawl in Boiling Fork.

Neither rider even glanced back as they swung the corner into Main and rode on for the depot, which they reached just in time as the stage from the south wheeled in to deposit the handsome young man carrying a shiny black valise.

It was no secret in town that Barlow King had allegedly forced his daughter to invite the man she had been seeing occasionally for the weekend. Nor were there few who could be unaware of the underlying reason for the big man's actions. The way King had come to see things, if Cassie was going to marry money, better sooner than later, all things considered.

Wilson didn't understand how rich folks lived their lives, and he understood even less when he and Brogan were given the job of escorting a pale-faced Quentin Kaley back to the depot just on dusk to catch the southbound stage.

They'd left their employer at the mansion, redfaced with rage and swallowing whiskey by the tumblerful. His desperate plan had failed and his daughter had given her would-be suitor his marching orders.

By next morning, Barlow King had announced the closure of the Monte Cristo Mine and the first major riot had erupted as a result.

* * *

Cole Shannon was alone in the corral with the new colt when he saw Quade emerge to stand on the side porch and stare off in towards the town trail.

Turning his head in that direction, Shannon sighted the horseman coming down to the title gate, a slender figure astride a flashy bay gelding.

Courtney Riley had been away overnight, where he didn't know. He was glad to see him safe and sound in light of the ongoing violence and bloodshed currently gripping the town.

He turned at the sound of steps and greeted Quade with a nod.

'Nice day, Jack.'

'Uh-huh.' Quade leaned his arms on the corral fence and eyed the colt. 'He learning anything yet?'

Shannon smiled. 'Not a lot, I guess. Not as much as he should, that's for sure.'

'Typical young 'un,' the other replied, turning his head to watch Riley coming across the flats.

'You still sore at the boys, man?' Shannon asked, stroking the colt's silky neck.

'I guess.'

'I don't want you feeling that way. They were the best a man could have riding at his side in the war, but this is different. They've got oats to sow and places to see — '

'They're a pair of hotheads who'll come to grief without us older heads around to steer them straight, and you know it as well as I do, Shan!'

Shannon stared. That was a big speech for taciturn Jack Quade. 'Man,' he said, 'one of the great things in life is being free to make your own mistakes. Me, I'm hoping Kit and Court will just cut loose, raise some hell, maybe take a few hard knocks, and then come back and maybe decide ranching's not a bad way to live after all.'

'Sounds like a big maybe to me . . . ah, hi there, Court. Sick and hung over, I hope?'

Riley bounced out of the saddle and laughed. 'Same old Jack — thirty-two going on sixty-four.' He threw a phantom punch and turned to Shannon. 'What's doing, Shan?'

'The usual. How are things in town?'

'Bad and getting badder. I'm usually first in line for a good ruckus but what's going on in there just ain't any kind of fun. Since they shut down the mine there's been nothing but fights and busted windows. I tried to get Kit to come along but he's sparking some dancer and — '

'Or was,' Quade cut in, pointing. 'Look.'

It was Kit Quill arriving at the gallop, as usual. Shannon stroked his jaw. Things had to be bad in Boiling Fork if rawhide Kit wasn't enjoying it any more.

'Let's go get some breakfast,' he suggested, giving the colt a final rub before quitting the corral. 'Pop was threatening to cook some eggs he got in town yesterday, and I'd reckon you two town-cowboys would be about ready for something solid?'

Quill swung in to join them as they headed up the gradual slope to the ranch house, and the start of what turned out to be a memorable day.

There was nothing structured or pre-planned about it, just a laid-back sort of day when nobody felt much like working or doing much of anything in particular other than to sit about drinking coffee and yarning while waiting to see what Pop might whip up next on the rickety old stove.

The shadow of Riley's and Quill's eventual departure manifested itself occasionally, but was largely ignored until it went away. Even so, Shannon sensed the time was drawing close, suspected the two might have already pulled up stakes with their cut of the gold but for the worsening situation in Boiling Fork.

The two would be sorely missed, but he didn't want to think about that. So the long afternoon wore on and might have lasted until dark, but dusk brought the arrival of one of the servants from the King mansion.

The rider brought a message from Miss Cassie for Shannon; she would like to see him if he could maybe make it into town.

Shannon nodded soberly despite a sudden twinge of concern. Cassie had told him of her father's invitation to Quentin Kaley to come visit, and he was aware of what that could imply.

The rich young man sounded like a genuine catch and Shannon wished them luck, or at least pretended to. He did not regard himself as husband material, although if he were, King's daughter would likely be his first and only choice.

Once they realized he was set on riding in, the others decided to join him in light of the situation in the town.

As they dressed and readied their horses, Riley and Quill stood together on the gallery with folded arms on the railing, watching.

'Not coming?' called Digger Morgan. He winked. 'Could be easy to pick a fight, the way things are. Doesn't that tempt you, boys?'

'Any other night, Digger,' Riley called back with a touch of wistfulness. 'Hey, Shan, tell that good-looking woman if she gets tired of wasting her time with old geezers, there's a good-looking stud out here who'd give her the time of three or four lifetimes if she was to give him the eye!'

'Right!' Shannon called back, and turning his horse away from the hitch rail, looked at Pop Harney. 'They're fixing to leave,' he said quietly.

'Huh? How can you be sure?'

'I just am, is all.'

'Well, are you just gonna let 'em?'

'Best this way, Pop. No big goodbyes. They can get their share of the gold and ride out without any fuss, and I reckon that's how it should be.'

'Jeeze!'

'That's right, old-timer. C'mon, we've got miles to cover.'

The riders started off at the trot and quickly broke into a lope. Shannon looked back once to see the two still standing there on the gallery, watching them recede from sight.

★　★　★

Standing upon the flat roof of the bakery with a cigar clenched in his teeth, Lucky Ned Pepper clapped his hands and danced a little jig as a freshly lit fire began to blaze in an alleymouth nearby.

'Lordy, but I do love me a good old-fashioned Friday night wingding!' the killer laughed. 'What's the betting that by right about now, old moneybags Barlow King will be wishing he'd spent some of what cash he's got left on a stage ticket out of here. Wouldn't surprise me if those woolly-headed Cousin Jacks don't burn that big flash house down around his ears before the night's out.'

The clutch of sober-faced citizens sharing his patch of rooftop weren't sharing the newcomer's enjoyment, although most tended to agree with his words. The ongoing clash between the mine boss and his fired workers did appear to be heating up to a dangerous level as twilight tinged a smoky sky.

The bakery stood a good safe distance from the huge house, which was being protected from the drunken miners by King's full force of employees. This contained an impressive kernel of hard men all sworn to loyalty and all under the direct control, not of Barlow King, but of his high-priced lieutenant, Jet Brogan.

Brogan was everywhere tonight, shifting personnel from one hot spot on the perimeter to another, bawling orders that carried clearly over the racket and the shouting of the drunks, leading the occasional mounted sortie into the enemy ranks with telling effect.

The Days of Glory saloon had been converted into a casualty station back on Main and word had just circulated that a miner who'd been shot earlier in a virtual one-man drunken assault on the big main gates of the mansion, had died and another appeared in danger of joining him.

The sheriff was doing what he could to restore law and order — at a distance. Any time brawling erupted too close to the badgeman's position he was seen to shift — further from the besieged house every time.

A loud crash sounded and a roar

went up when the attackers realized that someone had driven a fire wagon into the main gates, doing considerable damage.

A man aboard the vehicle sprang from it, seized a grip on the gates and began to climb over, showing remarkable athleticism fired up by John Barleycorn.

Despite the missiles being hurled at him from the defenders' ranks, the man made it all the way to the top, and was vigorously climbing over when a warning cry went up and a slatternly woman on the fringe of the trouble screamed, 'Git down, Charlie, there's Brogan a-comin'!'

The climber turned his head to see the fast-moving rider coming up the west side of the house. The physique and carriage of King's personal bodyguard was unmistakeable. His bravado gone in an instant, the would-be invader threw a leg over the top bar of the gates again and was several feet below the top when the horse stormed by and Brogan's .45 roared like a cannon.

The climber crashed to earth and never moved again.

For a time it seemed the wrath of the mob would see the defenders swept away, and Lucky Ned jumped up and down like a kid at a noisy party, urging both sides on, not giving a rap who won just so long as there was blood and excitement to fire the spirit.

Yet the moment the fierceness began to ebb the killer's excitement faded. He turned his back on the mansion and looked sharply about him, searching for his henchmen.

'Over here, Pepper!'

The voice belonged to Navajo Joe, who was too proud to call anybody mister.

Pepper spotted the man with two more of his bunch. He jumped on to the ladder and swiftly clambered down it to join them.

By which time he was all business. 'Let's go. We've got to get out to that

High Tumbleweed tonight and find out whether they've got it out there with them, or not. We ain't waiting any longer, so let's hustle.'

As they headed for the livery Pepper, now as grim and sober as a hanging judge in contrast to his earlier excitability, shot a last glance back to see a general drifting back from the fence line of King's great house.

He sneered. The dead guy had scared the big hairy miners! Small wonder King treated them like dirt. They were!

They were crossing Goodpasture Street when Fletch suddenly clutched Pepper's sleeve.

'What?' snapped Pepper, coming to a halt.

'Yonder!' the tall man said, pointing. 'Ain't that him?'

'Him? Who the hell is him? I — hey! It *is* him. And he's brought his bunch with him.'

Riding directly across Main and making towards the trouble, were the men from High Tumbleweed Ranch:

Shannon, Morgan, Quade, Harney and Gar Brothers.

Five, not seven.

The outlaws waited expectantly but there was no sight of either of the remaining two.

'Showed up to play hero to that skirt!' Pepper panted. 'So, who ain't with him? That cocky bastard, for sure.'

'Riley,' supplied Poker Bill. 'The other one that ain't there's gotta be the kid with the long hair — '

'Quill,' supplied Navajo Joe. 'What do we — ?'

'This gets better and better,' Pepper cut him off, swabbing nervous sweat from his face. 'If those two young geezers are still out there when we show up, then we won't have to rip the dump apart looking for our gold, we'll persuade them to tell us!' He clenched his fists and turned his grinning face to the skies. 'Yeeehahhhh!'

Lucky Ned Pepper could be equally unpredictable whether elated, as he was now, or when one of his 'whalebone' moods overtook him — whalebones were at the bottom of the sea.

Moments later the main street of Boiling Fork lay empty under the stars. Hoofbeats rose and fell. Soon the first stragglers from the siege began trickling into sight and eventually the trickle became a flood.

There was still a storm of loud talk and dire threats but everyone knew the intimidating arrival at the siege site of the men from High Tumbleweed had put a limit on their mischief. For now.

10

Requiem Guns

Courtney Riley took a deep draw on his cigarette and stared across the table at Kit Quill.

'What?' Quill grunted. The night was getting on and the youthful pair were not accustomed either to being at the ranch at night or to being in the town, which they were finding more and more to their liking these days.

Riley flipped his butt into the dying embers of the grate fire and got to his feet. Quill was familiar with his close pard's every mood and state of mind, yet tonight good-looking Courtney seemed to have something totally different working on him; what it was he couldn't tell.

Then Riley said, 'Let's do it.'

'Huh?'

Riley made an impatient gesture. 'The gold. You heard Shan. They've got it all counted out and packed up for us out there. If that ain't telling us to go then at least it's inviting it, which is about the same thing. For mine, I'm up to here with cows and living in the sticks and — '

'All right — OK,' Quill broke in sharply.

Riley stared. 'You mean you agree?'

Kit Quill was on his feet, expression resolute. 'Man, it's going to be like losing an arm to quit the Brigade . . . but yeah, right now I'm ready to do it.'

Minutes later two dark figures emerged from the ranch house and started across the wide house yard. They stumbled some for the moon had been swallowed up by cloud an hour earlier and the night was black as the pit.

Riley stopped off at the old barn where he paused long enough to grab an old oil-lamp and touch it into life with a vesta. Excited now, they hurried into the overgrown swale until the windlass of the old well showed up in the light.

It was the work of brief minutes to draw the covering weeds away. Holding the lamp aloft they stared down to see two smaller grips resting upon the larger satchels beneath.

'Just as Cole said . . . ' For a moment Riley's face showed uncertain. He looked at the other. 'Jeeze, do you reckon we're doing the right thing — ' He broke off sharply. 'The hell with that! No second guessing. We know what we want to do and got to do. Here, grab my hand while I reach down and haul them up . . . '

Within minutes it was done. All that remained to be done was to re-cover the cache carefully and head back for the house, just as the moon reappeared high overhead. A brilliant, all-revealing full moon.

★　★　★

Sweat ran down Poker Bill's ugly face. 'Damnit!' the outlaw hissed, 'What in hell are they doing now?'

Navajo Joe adjusted his binoculars and focused them upon the ranch house below once again. Lights showed at the High Tumbleweed a quarter mile below their look-out position, and as the tracker adjusted the setting-screws, the figures of the two men on the gallery leapt into clear view.

'They dance.'

Poker Bill stared at the 'breed. 'Dance? Here, gimme a look, scalp-lifter.'

The one-eyed killer with the drooping black moustache snatched the instrument and put it to his eyes. Mostly, keeping watch on Shannon's spread as ordered by Pepper had been less exciting than watching grass grow. Tonight was proving dramatically different. Earlier on they'd seen five of the bunch leave for town, now the pair left at the house seemed to be acting like dingle-dodies in the night.

From what could be seen, one held a bottle to his lips while the other was clutching some kind of satchel to his chest and . . .

Poker Bill gasped and stared. For the man with the satchel had almost dropped it, and the watcher could tell just from the effort it took to catch it and lift it again that it was extremely weighty for its size.

He lowered the binoculars, knuckled his eyes then took another look. By this time the man with the satchel had tipped some of its contents on to a bench . . . and immediately there was the blink of lamplight on something golden.

'Judas!' he breathed. 'That's gotta be it!'

'What it?' growled Navajo Joe. He snatched at the glasses. 'Here, Joe look.'

He looked, he blinked his black rogue's eyes. 'Gold!'

'What'd I tell you?'

'W-what we do?'

Poker Bill was sweating profusely by this. Keeping watch on the spread each night the outlaws had been told to watch out for anything, any clue or sign that might lead them to the gold. Immediately convinced that they were seeing it now, he had to make a decision.

What would Lucky Ned do in this situation?

The answer was only too plain. Navajo Joe had already arrived at it, was on his feet and striding for the horses.

'Come, we go.'

'Go where?'

'Get gold.'

'But — '

'Get gold or Pepper shoot us. So? We go.'

* * *

They were repacking the opened satchel in the kitchen when Courtney Riley paused, glancing towards the open door.

'What?' said Quill, drawing the tie cord tight.

'Thought I heard something.'

'What's to hear out here but cows or coyotes? Let's get done and get riding, man.'

Riley bent over his satchel and neither heard nor saw anything untoward until the sixgun barrels angled through the open windows and opened up at point-blank range.

★   ★   ★

The ceremony was simple and moving. The preacher spoke well of the dead, lamenting how they had been taken in their prime, hinting that the double deaths on High Tumbleweed were symptomatic of all the other violence and ills currently besetting their town.

Later at the long bar of the Stagecoach saloon the mood was sombre, with rage simmering just below the surface.

'I still say they must have been professionals,' Gar Brothers reasoned. 'I mean, to get in that close without the boys being alerted, leaving no sign . . . not even horse-tracks.' He nodded grimly. 'Professional killers, for sure. Don't you reckon, Cole?'

But Shannon made no reply. Strange: he had lost more men than he ever wanted to remember during the war. But nothing prepared a man for losing friends. It simply wasn't something a man ever got used to.

He stared into the back bar mirror and didn't even see his pale reflection looking back at him. The shock was receding and he was beginning to think clearly. Reconstructing the events in his mind, he could only assume the headquarters had been under watch all along, and that the bloody strike had to be connected with the gold.

They'd shifted the remainder of the cache to another location since. But somehow no one seemed even vaguely interested in the gold any longer. They were like him. They could only think in terms of vengeance.

But where to begin?

'King?' Digger Morgan speculated, as though reading his thoughts.

'Huh?' Shannon straightened, coming out of his dark reverie. 'Hell man, why him?'

'The daughter and her beau . . . and you drawing the blame for busting up the romance. That cost King mebbe a son-in-law along with a whole heap of financial backing.'

'King's a son of a bitch, but he's not loco. Anyway, it was the boys who got shot, not me.'

'The killers could have just made a mistake — '

'Look, I appreciate your help, Dig, but you're on the wrong track. King is no saint, but this was outlaw stuff . . . I keep telling you they were professionals.'

'OK, just say we work on that notion. Where do we start looking? Half those half-starved Cousin Jacks look to me like they'd shoot their own mothers, but I don't see them as cold-blooded pros. Where are you going to find that breed in a hick town like this?'

'I can tell you I've already glimpsed one or two new faces in town that look like they could be fast guntippers, maybe even owl hoot . . .'

'You're only seeing them that way on account it's what you want to see.' Morgan clapped him on the shoulder. 'C'mon, let's get back to the spread, huh? Too mournful here.'

'Maybe after another. Barkeep! Another round, and keep them coming.'

'Hey, you said we'd just have one more.'

Shannon's face was grim as he picked up his glass. 'I lied.'

★ ★ ★

The huge room lay in deep gloom despite the sunshine flooding down outside. Barlow King had ordered the servants to keep the blinds drawn and had just uncorked his second flask of French brandy even though it was still only mid-morning. Slumped in a deep leather ottoman with his shirt unbuttoned, Boiling Fork's premier citizen looked like hell.

By contrast, the man standing across by the doors from where he could keep watch on the forecourts of the mansion below, stood upright, square-shouldered and healthy-looking as a stud bull.

Nothing ever affected Brogan. Nothing.

'What do we do now?' King's voice was low. The big man rarely let himself go, but now was such a time. 'What's left?'

'You could try the bank again, Mr King.'

'They wouldn't loan me squat. That rich boy was my last chance, and that's blown away on the wind. The miners want to lynch me and maybe that wouldn't be such a bad thing, come to think of it. No more worries . . .'

'Might be an idea to quit drinking and come up with some new ideas, boss man —'

The gunman broke off and grabbed his gun handle as a tap sounded on the double doors.

It was only the maid.

'I'm sorry, Mr King, but you told me to tell you if Miss Cassie should leave the house and — '

'Where has she gone?' King rumbled, forcing himself to sit upright. His expression was bitter. 'What new way has she come up with to shame and ruin the father that loves her? Well, speak up, woman.'

'She's gone, sir.'

'Gone? what do you mean — gone?'

'The yardman says she went riding, he doesn't know where. But he did say she appeared to be heading north . . .'

'North?' King was on his feet. 'That damned girl usually rides out to visit her precious deadbeats at the ghoster, but that's not north — '

'The High Tumbleweed's north, Mr King,' Brogan cut in.

King paled. He lumbered to his feet, spilling some brandy. 'By God and by

Judas, as if that girl hasn't caused me enough — ' He broke off and stared across at Brogan as a fresh notion struck home. A brutally unwelcome one. 'You don't think she could possibly be serious about that . . . that nobody, do you, Jet? After dumping Kaley and breaking my heart? Him?'

'It could be.'

'That all you have to say?'

'No. I'm asking you what do you plan to do about it, Mr King?'

'What . . . ?' For a moment the big man appeared confused; the blows were landing too swiftly today. Then he went to a window, ripped the drapes aside and sucked in a deep breath. 'Go tail her!' He sounded strong again. Resolute. 'See if she goes there, and if so, what she does. I tell you, Jet, if there is something going on between her and that nobody we might have to take steps. Know what I mean?'

Brogan nodded. He knew well enough. When cornered or threatened, Barlow King could play the game as ruthless as any man he knew, even himself.

★   ★   ★

Shannon paced the length of the gallery, turned and came back. Seated on the steps or leaning against the walls, the others watched him, Harney, Brothers, Quade and Morgan. The Five — the Seven no longer.

He halted to stand with hands on hips facing them. They'd not seen him look this grim since the dark days of the war.

'We're getting rid of it,' he stated flatly.

Silence.

They'd all expected a major decision in the wake of the killings, but their thoughts had been more focused on tracking down those responsible and dealing with them — Brigade style. But getting rid of the treasure?

Digger made to speak but Shannon motioned him to silence with a curt gesture.

'This is only my decision. Nobody has to agree. But that gold leaves the spread tonight no matter what. If anybody wants to go with it, you're free to do so. But if they go they don't come back. That's how it has to be. That gold worried me from the first day on account I've seen too often what it can do to men. And look what it's just done to us. It just about broke us up with Court and Kit, and then they got killed because of it. I hate that stuff and won't be losing any more sleep over it. Getting rid of it won't bring the boys back, I know, but it might save the rest of us before we're done.'

He broke off sharply, then made a sweeping gesture such as they'd often seen in wartime when their lives had hung in the balance behind enemy lines.

'OK, that's it. Talk it over and make a decision. I've given you mine. I'll be down at the barn.'

It was a half-hour later before he heard steps. A sober Pop Harney appeared in the doorway. 'We've made a decision, Cole.'

'And?'

'We're with you.'

'Everyone?'

'Unanimous vote.'

It was a moment Cole Shannon would long remember. He was pumping Pop's hand and telling himself he was feeling he was almost coming back to normal again, when, sighting movement he glanced out to see Cassie King riding in for the house on her piebald pony.

He ran to greet her. Didn't just walk, ran.

★ ★ ★

Lucky Ned possessed many aggravating habits. One was to keep people guessing about what he might be thinking. That was the way he was operating today. But the gang was letting him get away with it as they sprawled a round the big centre table in the Days of Glory, watching him pace to and fro, chain-smoking and silent, sure signs of something brewing.

They were in the money — to a degree. But there were surely prospects of still more to come, providing Ned could come up with a plan.

They had recovered roughly a third of the gold they'd chased half-way across Texas. But they wanted the lot and honestly believed they'd earned it, every cent. Yet they could understand Pepper not rushing a reckless decision right now. Earlier in the day they had seen those five from High Tumbleweed on the streets after the funerals looking like they wanted to kill somebody — anybody maybe. These killers didn't scare easy, but they weren't crazy-reckless either.

When Pepper eventually quit pacing and stopped to stare at them, they could tell he had decided upon something.

'It's out there and all we have to do is find it,' he announced.

They stared. Was that the best he could come up with?

It wasn't.

'I ain't scared of no man,' he went on, 'but I'm not forgetting the chase those bastards gave us, or the way they carved up the boys at Cracker Creek neither. We've nailed two of them and got a good chunk of the gold, but there's still five of them left. And now that they're mad and double alert they're going to protect what's left of that *dinero* something fierce, you can bet on it. So, do you know what we do?'

They had no idea. But he did.

'The girl.'

They stared. What girl?

'King's daughter, of course. That Shannon has fallen for her even if he mightn't know it yet.' He tapped his temple. 'But I saw the way he looked at her during the ruckus at the mansion, and that big geezer is gone whether he knows it or not. So we snatch her, get Shannon's bunch chasing all over searching, and while he's doing that, we get busy.'

'Doing what?' Poker Bill queried.

'Searching that spread, moron. We know the stuff is there . . . and how smart could a bunch of dumb ex-soldiers be at hiding anything?'

Some began to argue but were quickly silenced. For despite his self-assurance, Lucky Ned Pepper could see difficulties in his plan, uncertainties. But it was all they had, time was rushing by, and so they would go with it. Why so? Because he was Lucky Ned, was why. End of argument.

★　★　★

Marlowe was stiff and saddle sore towards the end of the day. The Treasury agent had covered a lot of territory riding around Boiling Fork and its surrounds, had travelled as far as the old ghost town and later made a long and careful survey of High Tumbleweed ranch from the high trail.

Plainly High Tumbleweed was involved in something big. A double killing had taken place out there the previous night and he'd sensed something hatching out there today, from what he'd observed. Even so, by the time he'd dismounted in the rear yard of his hotel he still felt largely dissatisfied with his day.

The Pepper bunch was still very visible about town and he'd heard more trouble was brewing along at the King mansion. But these were fragments and bits and pieces. He wasn't getting anything to jell or to suggest his next move. And, most important of all, where his gold might be.

Whenever Treasury's top manhunter was assigned a contract such as this, his first move always was to establish where the wealth in question was located, after which he would sit down to figure out the smartest way to transfer the said money or gold from the criminals to himself. Once he had his operational plan clear in his mind he would then set out to nail the guilty, but the cash always rated first priority.

Soaking large pale feet in soapy water in his crummy room, Marlowe sighed and stared from his fly-specked window. He noted all the houselights were blazing up at the King mansion on the next block. He sighed. Plainly he must look into that situation and its personnel also, for at that moment he felt he could not exclude anybody from involvement with the gold.

He reached out and absently stroked the smooth shaft of his big Sharps rifle. That always made him feel better.

It was a long slow time before he stirred heavily and began hauling on his boots. He was a worn-out man in his mid-forties who sometimes felt he had been in the saddle and dealing with dangerous men across several lifetimes.

But there was always more to do and he would do it tonight. He put on his hat, picked up the rifle and quit the dreary room, floorboards creaking under his ponderous weight. The big rifle went with him, as always.

It was coming on dusk as Shannon and Cassie King strolled by the crooked creek. The ranch house was visible from here and someone was in the process of firing up the lamps. The decision they had made didn't seem to matter quite as much now as it had before. He knew why, of course. Cassie.

Her coming out here today to visit was one of the best things ever to happen to him, he mused. Somehow she must have realized that something had happened between them at about the same time that that bright light had switched on for him also. Of course, he was aware she'd needed to escape the mansion, but selecting High Tumbleweed as her destination was surely a decision that had been meant to be made.

Although it was early days yet, he couldn't stop thinking of a possible future together, while at the same time being acutely aware of the possible obstacles to that.

Money would be one. She was accustomed to the best of everything, while he, regardless of how things evolved here today, would end up a relatively poor man. He'd like to stay on at High Tumbleweed should it prove possible, but even should he succeed in doing so, life here could scarcely seem an attractive proposition to any woman with a big-dollar background.

As they turned away from the creek to start back for the house, for the first time since finding the boys' murdered bodies in the front room of the house, Cole Shannon was beginning to feel strong again.

He had no awareness of hidden eyes watching from the higher ground to the north.

★　★　★

'What do you mean . . . they're riding?' Lucky Ned Pepper snapped. 'Riding where?'

'Well, Ned,' Fletch said slowly, 'kinda like headed west, I guess. Uh-huh, heading south of town by a back trail when I sighted them last, they was.'

'Which was where?'

'Well, after the bunch quit the spread, me and Joe here tagged them about five miles, then left Conneroy and Poker Bill tagging them while we reported back.'

'What else?'

'That's about it, Ned.'

'What about the freaking gold?'

'We never seen no gold, Ned. Just these fellas, the rich guy's daughter . . . and that beat-up old wagon.'

Lucky Ned Pepper was jittery with tension and mounting frustration. He liked to believe he was smart enough to be always a jump ahead. But on this long and brutal chase, and after having travelled such vast distances to wind up in this town where he felt sure in his water that the gold had to be, he'd appeared to run up against one dead end after another.

He couldn't get his head around what was happening today, was about to start in cussing to help ease the pressure on his brain, when he stopped rigid in the middle of the room.

Then he whirled upon the others and yelled, 'What freaking wagon?'

'Why, this beat-up old rig they were hauling along with them, boss,' Fletch said with a frown. 'Why?'

'That's it!'

The hellions exchanged glances. They weren't catching on.

So Conneroy asked, 'What is it, Ned?'

'The mother-loving, sin-and-corruption gold, of course,' came the emotional reply. 'All of them out there . . . all that toing and froing . . . and us knowing the gold is still there but not knowing just where . . . Don't you see? They realized they had to shift their stash after the shootings, and they're doing it . . . right under your dumb noses!'

'But, Ned — '

'Shut up!' Pepper hissed, striding for

236

the door. 'We're getting mounted, and if we don't pick up on their trail, then by God and by Judas you morons are gonna wish to God that . . . '

He let the threat hang as he vanished into the night. Four killers grabbed their hats and followed fast.

★ ★ ★

Brogan was weary. He'd covered long distances in his search for King's daughter before eventually catching a glimpse of the girl out on the High Tumbleweed Ranch. Unsure of what had been unfolding there, the hardcase had kept the spread under watch until sighting a group of people, including Cassie King, quit the acres and take the trail that angled west of the town.

The notion of simply bailing them up and demanding the girl return with him to the house occupied him for a time, but was ultimately rejected. He was a fast gun bolstered by supreme self-confidence. Yet going one-out against heavy odds involving men who'd already proved their mettle in the town, simply did not add up.

King was far better at figuring out plays than he was. Providing he was sober.

He was. Both sober and puzzled when the gunman made his report. But while the two were discussing what Brogan had witnessed, a hand rode in to report that on returning to base from a scout around the Monte Cristo, he'd sighted a party in the half-dark heading north-east of the mine in the direction of Bald Knob.

'Bald Knob?' King scowled. 'What in hell would they be doing out there? What's there but the old Number Two shaft?'

'Maybe we'd better go find out, boss man,' said Brogan, the man of action.

'Those newcomers . . . my daughter . . . going to Bald Knob by night?' King worried momentarily. Then he came to a decision, whirled and headed for the doors. 'You're right, and we'd better get out there. Fast!'

★ ★ ★

It was desolate out there, even by daylight, and a shadow-haunted and silent place under the pale starlight below Bald Knob where the abandoned Number Two shaft had been sunk a year ago. The second shaft had come about as a result of the dwindling of the Monte Cristo's copper reserves, when an expert decided there could maybe be another major seam to be uncovered out here three miles deep into the brush country.

The work had ceased only when it became clear there was no seam. The site had been left to erode slowly ever since.

Which made it just about perfect for their purposes, from Shannon's point of view, the old shaft being deep, remote, neglected and miles off the beaten track. Looking it over as his friends off-loaded the weighty load from the wagon, he saw how simple it would be to simply drop the gold to the bottom of the hundred-foot shaft, rake in a couple of tons of loose earth to cover it deep, blot out their sign and disappear.

Of course, he knew nothing was ever as simple as it might seem. Yet he still regarded it as the best of all possible prospects of getting shook of the gold without complications. And should it remain there undisturbed and undiscovered for all time, he believed that would be the ideal outcome for everybody, themselves in particular.

He was aware of nothing untoward in their hushed surrounds as he supervised the boys hauling the hessian-covered satchels towards the yawning hole. Heard nothing. Yet trouble had come amongst them, big trouble that snaked silently through brush and scrub, keeping low and with fingers curled around steel triggers while moonlight bathed the whole scene in its innocent light.

He was within ten feet of the shaft when the snarling voice reached him:

'Freeze or you're dead!'

His hand flew automatically to gun butt as he whirled. But he didn't draw, instead allowed his fingers to slide off the Colt handle the moment he saw them emerging from the brush, five hard-faced strangers, each with a gun in hand.

'Good catch!' One of them stepped forward, grinning as he spoke. He motioned them to ditch their shell belts and back up. Plainly the leader, he strutted like a gamecock and his black eyes glittered beneath his hatbrim. 'You know, I've heard of strange and sneaky folks hunting for gold in every spooky place where God's got land. But, you know, this is the first time I ever came across anyone heading out into the tall and uncut on a moony night to bury the stuff.'

He flicked his sixshooter at Shannon.

'That is what you are doing here, ain't it? Putting gold back into the ground?'

'What gold?' Shannon asked, playing

desperately for time. He was looking across at Cassie. She was white but held herself aloof and calm as she watched the hardcases gather up the discarded weapons and toss them carelessly into a pile. The gunmen kept turning to stare across at the dark bulk of treasure.

And Shannon thought: They know about the gold. But how?

'OK,' the leader said, his manner changing in a moment. Suddenly he looked as dangerous a man as Shannon had ever seen as he gestured with his sixgun. 'Line up along there yonder on the rim of the shaft.'

They were going to be killed! He was certain of it in that moment, for it was suddenly plain there in Pepper's glitter-dark eyes. And there was not a blind thing he could do about it. His eyes flew to Cassie as they began to move, and the irony of the situation was unbelievable. To have found this one woman after all the lonely years only to have it all torn away by scum such as this without even the chance to fight back . . .

He moved quickly to draw in closer to her to share their final moments, when the bellowing roar crashed out so close and unexpectedly that it sounded like a siege cannon at close range.

Shannon expected to fall and for those about him to go down with him. Someone did tumble. But it was not one of them but rather that pop-eyed redskin who leapt high into the air like a shot beast under the impact of a driving bullet, then crashed to earth as the surrounding brush erupted with gunfire.

With one thought only in mind Shannon hurled himself at Cassie, yelling to the others to get down as the night was filled with a cannonade of gunfire, whistling bullets and falling hellions.

Hurling Cassie to ground and dropping protectively across her body, Shannon saw a hawk-faced heller fall dead from a bullet in the brain, another slewing sideways with half his face blown away and screaming like a woman. He whirled, eyes snapping wide as the vast shape of a raging Barlow King emerged from the brush toting a bucking shotgun that blasted a killer's head into a crimson mush a split second before the tycoon was brought to the ground.

The stalwart shape of Jet Brogan dived to ground close by King and the bodyguard commenced fanning his trigger at the lightning shape of Lucky Ned Pepper whose luck held yet again as his bullets found the bodyguard who slumped over his smoking gun and moved no more.

It was a bloodbath more intense than anything Shannon had seen even in the war. And the guns were still raging as he dived ten feet to grab up a dropped pistol and shoot at a killer, who ducked and triggered back.

A moment later the killer stopped a bullet and went walking backwards on stiff legs, trying to focus on where the shot had come from, struggling to lift his smoking cutter and puzzled by his pain — dropping dead in his tracks when the hidden rifle roared again.

Who the hell else was firing from the brush?

Shannon got a bead on a lightning-fast Ned Pepper as the outlaw span to search for the hidden rifleman. As he did a figure that appeared to be ten feet tall in the moonlight emerged through the gunsmoke holding an enormous Sharps rifle at waist level and blasting shot after shot — a sportsman shooting clay pigeons.

The rifle churned once again with fierce and final authority and Lucky Ned fell like something that had never known life, his going just a faint rustling against the earth.

Shannon swung a smoking gun upon the towering figure as the man turned in his direction, body wreathed in gunsmoke.

'You won't need that pistol, Mr Shannon. I am the law.'

Shannon did not quite believe him. But he believed the man had saved both his life and others. And intensely weary in a moment now, he simply let the hot gun drop to ground.

Treasury agent Haig Marlowe nodded approvingly before turning to inspect the dead.

★　★　★

The federal marshals arrived by special stage from Pinto City late the following afternoon. Three of them. They were veterans who most often left the law books behind and instead arrived fully equipped with common sense, an instinct for fair play and good judgement, plus sawn-off shotguns in the event that they might be needed.

But the shooting was all over at Boiling Fork. In those final chaotic moments out at Number Two shaft, Ned Pepper and his dog-pack ceased to exist, and survivors were still lining up at Doc Watson's for injuries ranging from the trivial to one or two that might be life-threatening.

The marshals saw their duty in such situations as primarily to make an accurate assessment and then if possible reach a practical solution.

Sounded simple. Yet, veterans though they were, they were encountering some difficulties along the way when the medico got through patching up the big man from Washington, and Marlowe then presented himself to the lawmen to present a calm recounting of events leading up to the shoot-out.

Luckily Marlowe was known to the chief marshal, who gave him an uninterrupted hearing as the big man related the story of Lucky Ned's gold, of how it had come to be stolen by that outlaw in the confusion of the war's final days. This had led to the series of events of which the marshals had already been informed, culminating in virtually every last gold coin now being safely back in Marlowe's possession, which was the same thing as saying

Uncle Sam now had it tucked away safely in the hip-pocket of his blue-striped pants.

It soon became only too apparent to the marshals that whether or not the survivors and participants had all acted strictly in accordance with the law seemed to concern the Washington agent not at all.

The gunsmoke had cleared; Marlowe's eye was fixed firmly on the future.

'The killers and plunderers are gone and the gold is safe,' he summarized. 'Therefore I most strongly suggest that, considering what this community has already suffered, that the necessity of getting it back on its feet outweighs all other considerations. There is a community to rebuild, the mine is finished, the only citizen still with wealth is Barlow King who I do believe owes Boiling Fork virtually everything he possesses to compensate for his many crimes of exploitation. If Mr King can be 'persuaded' to accept this solution,

Marshals, I suggest you might consider waiving charges against him and elect someone of suitable experience and integrity to supervise the town's rebirth.'

★　★　★

They were the only people to see him off that bitter day three weeks later. Winter had come howling across Texas and by now Boiling Fork's violent Friday was already drifting into the past.

Shannon and Cassie King felt they were saying farewell to a close friend, as well they might. In the aftermath of the slaughter out at Bald Knob, Shannon had given Marlowe their side of the story honestly, beginning with Cracker Creek and winding up with the murderous finale here in which the Washington Treasury agent himself had played the dramatic major role.

He had felt certain that were he to be hauled before judge and jury for taking charge of valuables suspected at least of being stolen, his prospects of acquittal might have proved slim.

But Haig Marlowe both thought and acted in his own independent way. A score of times on his hunt the agent had feared it might well all come to nothing, that he might eventually be obliged to give it best and return to Washington empty handed.

But Shannon and his fighters had saved him from that outcome, and in return Marlowe had little trouble persuading the marshals to exonerate the Shannon Brigade's survivors officially of any culpability concerning the gold. They were then promptly invited to return for the big wedding when it came around.

But it was far too early to think of weddings or even of such challenges as helping rebuild the town's commercial strength and lay the ghosts of the past, as they would do.

For the present they simply had each other — the boys of the Brigade — and a grateful town with a future.

For a man whose one secret fear had been that he could finish up alone one day with just his memories, Cole Shannon considered all this a reward far greater than gold.

THE END

SILVER GALORE

John Dyson

The mysterious southern belle, Careen Langridge, has come West to escape death threats from fanatical Confederates. Is she still being pursued? Should she marry Captain Robbie Randall? The Mexican Artiside Luna has his own plans . . . With gambler and fast-gun Luke Short he murders Randall's men and targets Careen. Can the amiable cowboy Tex Anderson and his pal, Pancho, impose rough justice as with guns blazing they go to Careen's aid?

CARSON'S REVENGE

Jim Wilson

When the Mexican bandit General Rodriguez hangs Carson's grandfather, the youngster vows revenge, and with that aim joins the Texas Rangers. Then as Carson escorts Mexican Henrietta Xavier to her home, Rodriguez kidnaps her. The ranger plucks the heiress from the general's clutches, and the youngsters make a desperate run for the border and safety. Will Carson's strength and courage be enough to save them as he tries to get the better of the brutal general and his bandits?

INCIDENT AT COYOTE WELLS

Logan Winters

John Magadan escapes the hangman's noose, but his ride through the Sonora Desert bristles with violence and danger: he's pursued by Sheriff Tom Driscoll's posse; the Corson gang want the treasure which they feel they have been cheated out of; the Yaqui Indians want his horse and his blood. Beth Tolliver knows that Magadan holds the key to free her brother from Yuma prison — and something else . . . and she's decided that Magadan will stay to the bitter, bloody end.

THE MAVERICKS

Mark Bannerman

Despite his innocence, Adam Ballard had served eight years in prison. On release he returns to the Texas cattle ranch where he grew up. But his father is dead and his stepmother has remarried, and the past and present have entwined in a web of violence. Drawn into a bitter rivalry where guns blaze and men are lynched, Adam's past is part of the jigsaw of double-dealing, murder . . . and *Mavericking*, the illegal branding of other men's cattle . . .

THE GOLD MINE AT PUEBLO PEQUEÑO

Will Keen

In Del Rio, Johnny Dark, persuaded by stranger Nathan King, joins him in a deadly race to regain ownership of a gold mine. But nothing turns out the way King predicted. Five years later, to discover the truth behind certain tragic events, Dark rides to Del Rio with his wife, Cath. But he's immediately drawn into a gun battle against outlaws and the gold mine at Pueblo Pequeño — and the outcome is doubtful until the final shot is fired.

CATFOOT

J. William Allen

He had nothing on the guy — no name, no physical description, he didn't even know what crime he was guilty of! But Jim Catfoot, agent with the Pinkerton Detective Agency, knew that something was wrong. He'd got some questions he wanted answering. Mule-headed and using the few clues that he'd scraped together, he set about his task, unaware that this mission would put him on a countrywide chase — a chase that could only end in violent confrontation . . .